There was something about this man that brought out the passionate side of her.

Something that made Rose want him as badly as he seemed to want her. "Clint..." she murmured, splaying her hands across the broad surface of his chest. She felt the strong, steady beat of his heart beneath her fingertips. Saw his head lower, his eyes shutter. And then there was no more thinking, no more talking, only the masterful sensation of his lips moving over hers and the erotic sweep of his tongue.

He tasted like mint. He kissed like a man who always got what he wanted. And what he wanted right now, Rose realized, as his muscular frame pressed against her, was her.

The trouble was, she wanted him, too. And had from the first moment they had squared off under the hot Texas sun.

Dear Reader,

I admire entrepreneurs. Those among us who can see a need, brainstorm a way to fulfill it and then figure out a way to actually make it happen.

Rose McCabe is one of those self-made women. She took a need—finding a way to economically feed her triplets—then went to local farmers and cut a deal that soon benefited everyone in the community. For Rose, seeing any food go to waste is a crying shame. And that's why it's killing her to see a long-abandoned blackberry grove go untended, and even worse, *unharvested*!

Sexy former rodeo champion and cattle and horse rancher Clint McCulloch is the new owner of the land that luscious fruit resides on. He wants to mow the bushes down and turn the land back to pasture for his herd. Until Rose McCabe steps in and wheels and deals her way to a solution. One that Clint sees as temporary and Rose would like to last forever.

The real question is: Can Rose negotiate their way to love? Or is theirs a lifelong deal that will never be made?

For more information on this and other titles, please visit me on Facebook or cathygillenthacker.com.

Happy reading!

Cathy Gillen Thacker

LONE STAR DADDY

CATHY GILLEN THACKER

HARLEQUIN® AMERICAN ROMANCE®

Recycling programs
for this product may
not exist in your area.

ISBN-13: 978-0-373-75570-7

Lone Star Daddy

Copyright © 2015 by Cathy Gillen Thacker

Printed in U.S.A.

Cathy Gillen Thacker is married and a mother of three. She and her husband spent eighteen years in Texas and now reside in North Carolina. Her mysteries, romantic comedies and heartwarming family stories have made numerous appearances on bestseller lists, but her best reward, she says, is knowing one of her books made someone's day a little brighter. A popular Harlequin author for many years, she loves telling passionate stories with happy endings, and thinks nothing beats a good romance and a hot cup of tea! You can visit Cathy's website, cathygillenthacker.com, for more information on her upcoming and previously published books, recipes and a list of her favorite things.

Books by Cathy Gillen Thacker

Harlequin American Romance

McCabe Multiples

Runaway Lone Star Bride
Lone Star Christmas
Lone Star Valentine

McCabe Homecoming

The Texas Lawman's Woman
The Long, Hot Texas Summer
The Texas Christmas Gift
The Texas Wildcatter's Baby

Legends of Laramie County

The Reluctant Texas Rancher
The Texas Rancher's Vow
The Texas Rancher's Marriage
The Texas Rancher's Family

Visit cathygillenthacker.com for more titles.

Chapter One

"You can ignore me as long as you want. I am not going away." Rose McCabe followed Clint McCulloch around the big farm tractor.

Wrench in one hand, a grimy cloth in another, the rodeo cowboy turned rancher paused to give her a hostile glare. "Suit yourself," he muttered beneath his breath. Then went right back to working on the engine that had clearly seen better days.

Aware she was taking a tiger by the tail, Rose stomped closer. "Sooner or later you're going to have to hear me out."

"Actually, I won't." Sweat glistened on the suntanned skin of his broad shoulders and muscular back, dripped down the strip of dark hair that covered his chest, and arrowed down into the fly of his faded jeans.

Still ignoring her, he moved around the wheel to turn the key in the ignition.

It clicked. But did not catch.

His expression impassive, he strode back to the engine once more, giving Rose a good view of his ruggedly handsome face and the thick chestnut hair that fell onto his brow and curled damply against the nape of his neck. At six foot four, there was no doubt Clint was every bit as stubborn—and breathtakingly masculine—as he had been when they were growing up.

And, because he was four years older than she—which made him thirty-three now—likely feeling as if he were all the wiser. And more experienced.

Which, she determined fiercely, he was not.

She ambled close enough to see the darker rim of his sable brown eyes, then inclined her head at the engine. "Still not working, hmm?"

He grunted and muttered something she was just as glad not to be able to decipher.

Not above needling him if that was what it took to get his attention, she rocked back on the heels of her cowgirl boots and drawled, "Sure would be nice if you could afford to pay someone who knew what he was doing to fix that tractor. Or better yet, buy a brand new one."

She paused to let that idea sink in.

Pivoting away from him, she turned to look out at the thousand acres of Double Creek ranchland sprawled behind the big two-story ranch house, stable and barns. "Of course, maybe I should be thanking my lucky stars you not only haven't a clue how to get that machine up and running, but also are reportedly operating this ranch on a very thin margin. Because the combination of those two things—" she turned around to tip her hat back and give him a dazzling smile "—is going to keep you from bulldozing the hundred acres of beautiful blackberries on this property."

Finally Clint straightened. He looked her right in the eye. "Not necessarily," he said.

HIS UNINVITED GUEST was speechless.

Deciding the only way to discourage her was to let her know exactly where they stood, Clint continued. "I could always borrow a tractor from any one of my friends." *Ex-*

cept they were all using their tractors for spring clear-ing, mowing and planting. "And get the job done today."

Rose's pink lips slid into an astonished pout. "You wouldn't!"

Pushing aside the notion of what it might be like to taste the tempting softness of those lips, he moved his gaze back to her wide-set sage-green eyes and nodded tersely. "I most certainly would."

"But...you're sitting on a gold mine!"

He shrugged, letting his gaze linger once again over the delicate, feminine features of her heart-shaped face. "I'm sure you think so."

She drew in a breath. "Do you know how much four ounces of blackberries retail for these days?"

"Haven't a clue."

"Four dollars!"

He kept his eyes locked with hers in an attempt to in-timidate her into going away. "So?" To his mounting frus-tration, his maneuver did not achieve its goal.

Rose huffed. "The typical yield of mature plants like yours is five to ten thousand pounds per acre!"

Which meant—he quickly did the math—the total of a good yield would be anywhere from two to four million dollars, retail, for one crop. However, a farmer would get a lot less wholesale.

"If you can get them picked," Clint pointed out, forc-ing himself to be practical. He did not have the money for harvesting, either.

Grimacing, he paused to remove his Stetson and wipe the sweat gathering on his brow. "I can't."

Following suit, Rose swept off her straw cowgirl hat and slapped it against her sleek denim-clad thigh. Her un-ruly ash-blond curls glittered with golden highlights. The thick silky strands were cut to frame her face and rested against her chin. She ran the fingers of her free hand idly through her hair before placing her hat back on her head. "Actually," she countered, returning his impudent stare, "you could."

It was Clint's turn to heave a sigh of frustration. He straightened once again, aware they were talking about something that just wasn't going to happen.

"The point is—" he kept his gaze locked with hers "—I'm not interested in being a berry farmer. I'm a rancher. I want to restore the Double Creek Ranch to the way it was when my dad was alive. Run cattle, and breed and train cutting horses here." He pointed to the blackberry patch up for debate. "And those thorn- and weed-infested bushes are sitting on the most fertile land on the entire ranch."

Rose's expression turned pleading. "Just let me help you out."

"No." He refused to be swayed by a sweet-talking woman, no matter how persuasive and beguiling. He had gone down that road once before, with a heartbreaking result.

A silence fell and Rose blinked. "No?" she repeated, as if she were sure she had heard wrong.

"No," he reiterated flatly. His days of being seduced or pressured into anything were long over. Then he picked up his wrench. "And now, if you don't mind, I really need to get back to work…"

She stared at him a moment longer. Started to say something, then stopped herself, shrugged and walked off.

A little surprised the inimitable Rose McCabe had given up—just like that!—Clint watched the lovely entrepreneur climb into her extended-cab Rose Hill Farm pickup truck and drive away.

He tinkered with the tractor motor another half an hour, then gave up. Much as he hated to admit it, Rose was right about one thing. He was never going to be able to fix this engine on his own. So he went into the house, showered and changed into fresh clothes, grabbed his keys and wallet and headed to the farm- and ranch-equipment dealership in Laramie.

He had no trouble getting someone to wait on him, but he didn't like what Swifty Mortimer had to say. "Trying to find parts for a tractor that's forty years old is going to cost more than a new one," the salesman announced.

Clint braced himself for the worst. "And how much is that?"

"Several hundred thousand dollars. Of course, you can lease at a rate of five thousand dollars a month. Or buy used and reconditioned agricultural equipment, which will still likely run you into six figures."

Clint sighed. All options were well out of his range. He'd spent what cash he did have on hand adding to his herd of black Angus and buying more cutting horses, which now numbered six.

"Not going to work for you, hmm?" the salesman guessed.

Clint shook his head.

"Well, then, maybe you could work a deal with a friend."

"Or better yet," a familiar female voice said from somewhere behind them, "me!"

Clint turned to see Rose McCabe standing behind him, with the owner of the dealership, Jeff Johnston, at her side. An affable man in a sports coat and jeans, the forty-year-old bachelor was a well-respected Laramie County businessman with an eye for the ladies.

Realizing he was no longer needed, Swifty discreetly eased away to help another customer coming in the door.

Rose beamed at Clint. "I was just talking to Jeff about you."

Pushing aside an unexpected twinge of jealousy, Clint shrugged at whatever Rose was trying to finagle now. "Sorry she bent your ear, Jeff."

Jeff extended his hand to Clint. "Actually, I'm glad she did."

"Seems like you could do each other a favor," Rose commented when the two men had finished shaking hands.

Clint noted that Jeff seemed to think so, too. "Really. And how is that?" he asked dryly. His patience was beginning to wear thin.

Barely containing her excitement, Rose asked Jeff, "Why don't we just show him?"

The man smiled and gestured broadly. "After you…"

Rose settled her hat on her head and led the way back out into the late-spring sunshine.

On the corner of the lot sat a brand-new machine. As narrow in width as a lawn tractor but three times as tall, it had a glassed-in cab for the operator situated near the top and a produce catcher sticking six feet out to one side. A large vacuum hose fed into a belt-run crop sorting and processing system that ran the length of the entire machine, and there was a ledge for a produce box directly beneath the end of the produce catcher. Behind the tractor was a detachable flat-bed trailer with room for stacked produce boxes.

Cheerfully Rose explained, "You drive the berry harvester between the rows. The nylon bars enclosed in the top of the machine move through the bushes and gently shake the ripe fruit loose. The captured blackberries are drawn up through the hose at the bottom and move through the machine via conveyor belts, where any loose leaves, sticks and thorns are removed, and gently drop into the box below." She took a breath, then continued. "When the box is full, a sensor will sound. You stop the tractor, remove the full container and replace it with another."

It sounded pretty easy. And a lot less expensive and labor-intensive than picking them by hand. "Except there are no rows to drive through in that mess of blackberries on my property," Clint pointed out. The canes had grown together into a dense thicket years before.

Rose shrugged. "So we'll use a tractor to make some." She lifted a hand to cut off any objection. "Yes, you'll be mowing down some perfectly good bushes and blackberries in the process, but you'll still be left with a ton of plants and plenty of fruit in a much more manageable situation. And with a new set of berries ripening every two days for the next three to five weeks, depending on weather, that is a lot of berries, McCulloch."

And a whole lot of money, Clint acknowledged. Still, he hated being pushed into anything. "Let me guess." He narrowed his eyes at her. "You're just the person to take the blackberries off my hands?"

Oblivious to the amused way Jeff was watching her, she dipped her head in a playful bow. "I do run a wholesale Buy Local fruit and vegetable business and co-op at Rose Hill Farm."

Clint thought about what it was going to cost to get his cutting-horse breeding and training business off the ground. He was still running the fifty black Angus on a neighboring ranch and spending a lot more time than he liked giving cutting-horse riding lessons and hiring himself out as a cowboy just to bring in needed operating cash. It had been over a year since he'd repurchased the property he grew up on, and although he had no trouble meeting his mortgage payments, he was still a long way from making the ranch what he knew it could be.

He shook his head in frustration. He was tempted, but too smart to follow her down a trail that would most likely only set him even farther back in the end. "Look, even if I wanted to do this, there's no way I could afford this machine." The price label on the side stated it retailed for two hundred fifty thousand dollars.

Or about the same as the new tractor he needed but could not yet purchase.

"Actually, you can," Rose insisted smugly.

Clint scoffed. "What are you going to do? Loan me the money to lease it?"

Her grin widened. "Better than that. I've worked out an arrangement with both Jeff and Farmtech, the manufacturer."

Clint couldn't say he was surprised Rose had the owner of the dealership at her command. Or any red-blooded man with an appreciation for a smart, beautiful, sexy woman, for that matter.

"What kind of arrangement?" he couldn't help but ask. Jeff quietly excused himself and headed back in the direction of the office.

Now that they were alone beneath the shimmering blue Texas sky, Rose focused all her energy on Clint. "One that won't cost you a cent!" She stepped closer, persuading cheerfully, "All you have to do is use the berry picker on your property to bring in the crop. And then offer the required testimonial, which I will support and bolster in any way that's needed."

He studied her. "Okay, I see what's in it for you." She would get access to the blackberry crop she so desperately wanted for her wholesale produce business. He lowered his face until they were almost nose to nose. "But why would the dealership and the manufacturer agree to let me do this free of charge?"

Instead of stepping back as he expected, she came nearer, enticing him to inhale her sunny, citrus perfume. "Because this particular machine is a brand-new design, with very few willing to buy it thus far. Farmtech is hoping to change that via positive experience—especially here, because in Texas, most berries are still picked by hand."

It sounded simple enough, but his gut told him there

was more to it. He stepped back and studied her, glad they were no longer within kissing distance. "What *aren't* you telling me?"

She shifted her glance to the left, suddenly looking a little nervous. "That's pretty much it…"

"But not all," Clint surmised.

She cleared her throat and turned her attention back to him. "They also want to come out to the Double Creek Ranch and film you using the product. Of course, you'll get paid for your time and trouble at a rate commensurate with others working in the spokesperson industry."

No question, the additional money would help. But the thought of riding around on a berry picker in front of a camera bordered on the ridiculous. "You're kidding." Dread filtered through him. "You're *not* kidding."

"Well—" Rose wrinkled her nose. "You are a former rodeo star. And, well, if not all that handsome, at least not all that ugly…"

"Cute."

"And it wouldn't be your first endorsement."

Aha. Here comes the sales pitch…

Luckily this wasn't the first time a beautiful woman had used her charm to try and wheedle him into agreeing to something he had no business doing.

He rocked forward on the toes of his boots. She did the same on hers.

Letting her know with a glance she wasn't going to railroad him into anything, he said, "What few ad campaigns I've done have been for saddle soap and leather gloves. Nothing to write home about."

She aimed another sweet, tempting smile his way that had his lower half tightening, despite his vow to remain unaffected.

"Well, maybe this will be," she offered hopefully.

Silence fell.

Before the two of them could say anything more, Jeff strode toward them. He held a clipboard piled with papers in one hand, a pen in the other. "The film crew and publicity team will be here at some point during the next couple of weeks, provided we can get the papers signed and faxed back to Farmtech today."

Clint thought about the potential hassle and humiliation. He also thought about the income such a deal could bring in. And what that, in turn, could do for his plans for his ranch. Which was more important? His pride—or the future of the Double Creek?

Clenching his jaw, he asked, "What about the berry picker?"

Out of the corner of his eye, he could see Rose was so excited she was practically bouncing up and down.

"We can have it delivered to the McCulloch ranch by Wednesday," Jeff promised.

Two days from now. "And in the meantime...?"

"The dealership will loan you a tractor and tiller."

Rose smiled gleefully. "By tomorrow morning?"

Jeff nodded. "Just tell me what time you want it out there."

She turned to Clint. "9:00 a.m. okay with you?"

In for a penny, in for a pound. And given the fact he'd wanted to mow down all those bushes anyway—and did not have a working tractor of his own—Clint figured this would give him a head start. "Sure, why not." Jeff handed him a set of contracts that covered all manner of product endorsements and included an extensive general liability clause. Clint had expected it to be a generic fill-in-the-blank document. Instead, his name and address were preprinted on everything.

He frowned suspiciously at the two people standing opposite him. "How the heck did the manufacturer know I would say yes?" The company's legal department had set the first advertising component of the work to begin ten to fourteen days after signing. Which—he noted by the date on the documents—they had expected to be today?

Rose flushed guiltily.

It wasn't hard for him to jump to the next assumption. "You said yes for me?" Clint asked in disbelief.

Rose cleared her throat and made a dismissive gesture. "Tentatively. But only because I knew I could talk you into it."

Damn, but she had moxie.

The prettiest sage-green eyes.

And the softest, most kissable lips.

Oblivious to the nature of his thoughts, she defiantly stood her ground. "With the crop ripening any day, there was no time to waste. And it wasn't that big of a gamble. You're a businessman as well as a rancher. I figured it wouldn't take long for you to see the light. You'll get sixty-five cents from my operation per pound of fruit."

He stopped her with an imperious lift of his palm. "Make it a dollar."

She scowled. "Now, wait just a red-hot minute, cowboy! I still have to clean, sort, package and market the berries for you."

"Not to mention pick up and deliver," he added. "Since I don't have a produce truck, either."

She stared at him. "Seventy-five cents, McCulloch. And that's my ceiling."

He stared right back, then shrugged. "Done." He extended a hand.

Rose slid her palm into his. The sensation of her surprisingly soft and silky skin, coupled with the strength of her grip, sent heat pouring through his veins.

He hadn't been this aware of a woman in ages. If ever. And judging by the stunned look in her eyes, she was feeling the same.

He thought about how long it had been since he'd been close to anyone and swore silently to himself. What had they gotten themselves into?

Chapter Two

"What's wrong?" Rose demanded early the next morning.

How about everything? Clint thought, directing his full attention to the woman striding toward him. Although it was due to heat up later in the day, right now it was damp and cool. Rose had hooked a pair of sunglasses into the neck of her bright-yellow T-shirt and thrown a denim jacket over her slender shoulders. Snug-fitting jeans and boots covered her lower half. Her straw hat hid her cloud of ash-blond curls.

Not stopping until they stood toe-to-toe, she persisted, "Why do you have *that look* on your face?"

Clint cut a glance at the long line of pickups and tractors driving onto the Double Creek Ranch, then turned back to her, keeping his temper in check. "You really have to ask?"

She shrugged, her expression more innocent than the situation warranted. "I told you I'd get you a loaner tractor delivered today." She waved a hand in the direction of the tractor dealership flatbed leading the way. "And I have."

It looked like a nice one, too. Brand spanking new. With an air-conditioned cab, a fact he was sure to appreciate as the sun rose higher in the sky.

Clint jerked his head at the convoy. "And the rest of this?"

"Oh." Rose spared him a look. "I called in a few favors

to get other farmers in the area to help us make the rows. This way we can get it done in one day."

He lifted his brows. "You didn't think to ask me first?"

Her pause went on a second too long.

"Or you *did* think to ask and decided not to."

Another shrug and a small, mischievous smile. "I might have discovered—after I finished organizing everything last night—that it was too late to call you."

He narrowed his eyes, not buying that excuse for one hot second.

"Or...I might have had a feeling that you're one of those gotta-do-it-all-myself types." She became serious. "With the first of the berries ready to be picked tomorrow, we really don't have time to waste."

Uh-huh. Just as he had thought.

"Deal or not, Ms. McCabe, this is still my ranch."

"Oh, I am aware." Tossing her head, she lifted a lecturing finger his way. "But that doesn't change the fact you have agreed to sell those blackberries to me, McCulloch! Or in any way alter the fact that I, in turn, have promised those same berries to a number of local stores, as well as the members of the Rose Hill Farm co-op! All of whom, as it happens, know the importance of bringing a crop in at just the right moment."

He couldn't argue. Any berries left to fall on the ground were money down the drain. "You seem to have it all figured out."

A shadow fell over her face—as if he'd struck a nerve. "You'll thank me when I cut your first check."

He supposed he would, at that.

"In the meantime...how about getting off your high horse long enough to come and thank all the neighbors who have so kindly agreed to help us?"

Clint fell into step beside her. "I suppose I shouldn't have been surprised," he murmured, nodding at the farmers coming forward to greet him. "Laramie is a place where neighbors help each other out."

Rose smiled, sweetly this time. "You're darn right about that, cowboy. That's how we farmers and ranchers all survive."

"LOOKING GOOD AROUND HERE," Gannon Montgomery told Clint later that evening when the two met at the Double Creek to settle their monthly accounts.

Friends since childhood, both were back on the ranches where they had grown up. Clint paid Gannon a grazing and usage fee for running his cattle and cutting horses on Gannon's ranch—the Bar M. In return, Gannon paid Clint to keep up the pastures on his land and exercise and take care of his family's horses.

Moreover, Gannon was a prominent local attorney who was married to Rose's sister, Lily. So there was little about the McCabe women or Laramie County he did not know.

Clint turned his gaze to the neatly plowed rows between the thick, plentiful six-foot-tall bushes. "More like a blackberry farm or something out of the Napa Valley." Which was a far cry from the ranch he and his family had always intended it to be, before he and his siblings had been forced to sell during probate, after his parents' death, years ago.

He sighed. "But it will be easy to get the berry picker through." Although he wasn't looking forward to the tedious work of driving that tractor and hauling crates of produce around. He would be much happier on the back of a horse, or even out on the land repairing fence, than trying to care for the delicate fruit.

Nodding in agreement, Gannon followed Clint inside. "Rose seems happy."

Pushing the image of the feisty woman with the delectable curves out of his mind, Clint cracked open two beers. "Tell me about it."

They toasted each other silently and then sat down at the kitchen island. "She's wanted to get her hands on all those berries for years," Gannon told him. "It was such a shame, seeing them all go to seed."

Clint snorted derisively, aware he'd been able to side-step Rose's requests the year before, after acquiring the property, simply by not being around during the harvest season. "Had the birds not been given free rein with them, they might not have spread to the degree they have."

"I sense you're irritated with my sister-in-law?"

Clint chose his words carefully. "Let's just say I have never met a woman so determined to have her own way."

"Or as likely to get it by whatever means necessary," Gannon deadpanned. "But, as Lily would say, that's part of her sister's charm. Or it has been since she was left with three kids to bring up entirely on her own."

Clint paused to take that in. "Rose's ex-husband isn't involved?"

Gannon shook his head, his expression grim. "Barry walked away clean nearly three years ago, right after their divorce."

Clint exhaled. "That's rough."

"So you can understand, then, why Rose is as single-minded as she is."

"Because she has to be."

Gannon nodded.

Clint admired a woman who went all out to provide for her family. That didn't mean, however, that he had to like the way Rose went about her dealings with him. He'd been down this road before. Almost married a woman who didn't just love being in the midst of excitement and drama but created it wherever she went. No way was he getting involved with someone like that again. Even if it was a woman as beautiful and feisty as Rose.

The two finished their beers and traded invoices.

"When are you going to get your ranch up and running?" Gannon asked.

"If it all turns out the way Rose is predicting—" Clint was holding his breath on that one "—and I get even half the cash she is promising…I'm hoping for early fall."

And then it would be bye-bye to the farming he had never wanted to do—and renting out his neighbor's land—and hello to horse and cattle ranching on the Double Creek, the way it was meant to be.

In the meantime, he had to deal with Rose McCabe.

And the delivery of the berry picker from the tractor dealership the following day. It arrived, as promised, shortly after nine in the morning. Clint half expected Rose to be there, too.

She wasn't.

While the sunny May morning was unexpectedly quiet, Swifty unloaded the big machine from the flatbed trailer, showed Clint how to use it and took off.

Deciding maybe this wasn't so bad after all, Clint loaded up the machine with heavy-duty plastic fruit crates, turned the engine on and headed for the field.

He'd barely made it down one row when the next surprise came. And the quiet morning outdoors that he'd been looking forward to vanished. Just like that.

CLINT SUFFERED THROUGH the day only because he had promised Farmtech, the local dealership and the produce co-op that he would.

As soon as the day's activity concluded, however, he headed inside his ranch house to get cleaned up.

And then, determined to get a few things straight before anything else unexpected happened, he made his way to Rose Hill Farm.

Until now, he had seen Rose's seventy-five-acre property only from a distance. As he passed beneath the wrought-iron archway, he could not help but be impressed. The rolling green pastureland was surrounded by neat white fence. Stately oak trees lined the drive that led to a small white Cape Cod–style bungalow with a dark-gray roof, cranberry-red shutters and a pine door. A huge new red barn, emblazoned with the Rose Hill Farm logo, sat behind that.

Rosebushes bloomed on either side of the front walk.

Bracing himself for whatever came next, he moved up the broad stone steps leading to the house and rang the bell.

There was a struggle with the lock on the other side. Then the front door swung open. The smell of something incredibly delicious—cornbread maybe—wafted out. A tyke-size McCabe stared up at him.

"Mommy!" the preschooler bellowed at the top of his lungs. "It's a man!" He craned his little head back as far as it would go. "And he's real big!"

Compared to the little one, Clint felt big. Although, at six foot four, he felt that way often.

Something clattered loudly—like a dropped metal pan in the kitchen. "Stephen!" Rose called out, sounding upset. She rushed around the corner, her hands buried in a dish towel. "I told you not to answer the…" She skidded to a halt midfoyer. Swallowed, cheeks pink. "Clint."

Aware he had never seen her—or imagined her—quite so harried, he moved his gaze over her cloud of chin-length dark-blond curls. She wore no makeup that he could see but was absolutely gorgeous just the same. She had on jeans, sneakers, a flattering peach button-up blouse and a ridiculously frilly and flowery apron over that.

He resisted the urge to tell her about the smudge of flour on one cheek. He was here on business, he reminded himself sternly. "Got a minute? I need to talk to you."

She crumpled the dish towel in her hand. "Ah…"

Two little girls appeared at her side. "Mommy, I'm hungry!" said the first.

The other complained, "You *said* dinner was ready."

Rose assured them with a smile, "It is."

The children's anxiety allayed, she turned back to Clint and waved him forward. "Come on in. I don't think you've ever met my triplets," she said, shutting the door behind him.

"Kids, this is Mr. McCulloch. Clint, this is Stephen." Rose pointed to her son. Clearly all boy, with short brown hair and dark eyes, he was clad in jeans and a Longhorns football T-shirt. He was busy trying to climb up the stairs from the wrong side of the railing.

Rose plucked him off the risers and set him back on the foyer floor. A prodding lift of Rose's brow had Stephen obediently extending his hand. "Hello."

"Hi." Clint noted the boy had a surprisingly strong and confident grip.

Continuing her introduction, Rose pointed to the daughter clad in a denim dress and deep purple cowgirl boots. "Scarlet."

The little girl holding an open storybook had long, curly, strawberry-blond hair, green eyes and glasses.

Scarlet smiled at Clint sincerely. "Hello."

Clint grinned back. "Good to meet you, Scarlet."

"And Sophia," Rose concluded, gently guiding the shyest of the three children forward. Clad in a ruffled skirt, matching knit shirt and ballet slippers, the little girl had long, dark-brown hair that was straight and silky, and clear blue eyes.

She shook Clint's hand mutely.

"Nice to meet you-all," he said.

Stephen muscled his way to the front. Unable to stand still, he put his weight on one leg, then the other, peering up at Clint curiously all the while. "We're three and a half."

He gestured importantly at himself and his two siblings. "How old are you?"

Rose jerked in a breath and lifted a chastising palm. "That's *not* a question we ask grown-ups. Not ever. Remember?"

If there was one thing Clint remembered, it was how insatiably curious he had been at the same age. "I don't mind." He looked back at the kids. "I'm thirty-three."

"Mommy's twenty-nine," Scarlet announced.

"And a half," Sophie said.

Rose blushed again.

Letting their gazes collide, then linger, Clint said, "Good to know."

Looking adorably flustered, Rose whirled away from him, then made a little shooing motion with her hands. "Just let me get them seated." Her kids darted through the hall, past the corner, and into the cozy space at the rear of the home. Comprising almost all of the first floor, it was at once kitchen, casual dining and living area. "And then—"

"Do you like mini-corndog muffins, Mr. Clint?" Stephen interrupted.

If the golden-brown confections were half as good as they smelled and looked, heck yeah.

"It's bite-size cornbread with very small chunks of wiener tucked inside," Rose explained. "A kid-friendly version of a corndog without the hazard of a stick in the center."

"'Cause if you do like them," Scarlet said, taking charge, "we can share. That's polite, isn't it, Mommy?"

Rose swiped a hand across her face, spreading the aforementioned flour from her cheek to her ear. "Sweetie, I don't think we want to put Mr. Clint on the spot."

Trying not to think how long it had been since he'd had lunch—had he stopped to have lunch?—Clint cut the reluctant hostess off with a smile, knowing it would irritate her. He owed her that. He pulled up a chair at the round oak table. "Thanks. Don't mind if I do," he drawled.

"You really want to have dinner. With us?" Rose clearly enunciated every word, giving him time, it seemed, to come to his senses.

He shrugged, figuring laying down the law to her could wait a little while longer. At least until he had part of his appetite sated. "Unless there's not enough?"

ROSE COULDN'T PLEAD THAT, much as she might like to. With three kids and herself to feed, and the closest restaurant a good twenty minutes away, she always made enough to feed an army.

"Of course there is." It was having him underfoot, looking—and smelling—so ruggedly handsome and sexy, wreaking havoc with all her senses that was the problem. A fact he seemed to know darn well, judging by the pure masculine devilry in his smile.

A tingle of awareness swept through her. Firmly ignoring it, she went back to get the rest of the serving dishes. She had promised herself she wasn't going to ever let her sensual side rule her life again, after her ex-husband had left her and the kids. She meant it.

"What about green beans?" Stephen asked, making a face at the bowl she set in the center of the table. "And celery? Or carrots?"

"Do you like *those*, Mr. Clint?" Sophia asked.

"Because we don't like any of them!" Scarlet declared.

Clint looked at Rose. She doled out two muffins per child, as well as a carrot stick, a piece of celery, and two green beans. "Slight aversion to v-e-g-e-t-a-b-l-e-s these days," she explained.

Wasn't that ironic, given what she did for a living.

Sophia rested her chin on her hand and stared at Clint,

warming up to him with surprising quickness despite her shyness. "Yeah, we don't like veggies."

"So much for spelling it out," Clint quipped.

Rose mugged at him comically. Then she brought an extra place setting for Clint. Serious once again, she told her children, "You may not remember it now, but all three of you *did* like veggies when you were little. And you would again if you would just try them with an open mind."

"Nope. We won't," all three kids said, their heads shaking stubbornly in unison.

The doorbell rang again.

Not exactly unhappy about the reprieve—she didn't know what it was about Clint that had her tingling all over every time she saw him—Rose lifted a hand. "I'll get it."

Leaving the kids and Clint to entertain each other, she rushed toward the door. And was surprised to see Miss Mim and Miss Sadie on her front porch, from the Laramie Gardens retirement-home complex.

"We heard about the berries," Miss Mim enthused. As always, she was dressed in an outrageously colorful outfit that clashed with her flame-red hair. "Any chance we could get some tonight?"

Looking as elegant as always, Miss Sadie smiled. "We're having an ice cream social."

Rose grinned. "No problem. If you want to head for the barn, I'll catch up with you." She dashed back to the kitchen.

Clint was sitting with the kids, mischief gleaming in his eyes. Rose didn't know what had been said, but they were all laughing as if he were the most charming guy on earth. Relieved, as well as a little peeved she had missed out on the hilarity, she asked him, "Would you mind watching them for a couple of minutes while I take care of something?"

He smiled genially, as relaxed as she was stressed. "Sure."

She raced out, still a little stunned to find the four of them getting along so well.

The lonesome cowboy was always so grumpy and contentious around her! Who would have thought he would enjoy being around her kids?

NO SOONER HAD the front door shut behind their mother than the kids jumped down from the table. Clint watched as two of the triplets ran toward the fridge. The other disappeared into the pantry. "Whoa now," he said, beginning to feel a little alarmed. Especially since he sensed they wouldn't be doing whatever this was if their mother were still on the premises. "What's going on?"

Stephen yanked open the fridge door so hard he nearly fell over. "I'm getting the ketchup."

Sophia stuck her head out of the pantry just long enough to declare, "I want honey."

Scarlet shoved her brother aside. "I want mustard."

They carried their trove back to the table.

Clint got up to shut the refrigerator, then the pantry door. By the time he returned to the table, they were struggling to get the squeeze bottles open. Because Stephen was closest, Clint moved to assist him first. "Let me help you with that."

The tyke jerked away, the bottle clutched firmly in his small hands. "I can do it!"

Clint eyed the red bottle. It seemed pretty full. "Really, I—"

Squirt.

A spray of red flew past Stephen's plate and hit the center of the table instead.

"Ah…" A word that shouldn't be used around children nearly slipped from Clint's lips, but thankfully did not.

Determined to react as calmly and patiently as he was sure Rose would, Clint started to reach for the bottle. Before he could get it, Scarlet squirted the mustard with all her might, with equally messy results. Sophia was no better at dispensing the honey.

This time Clint did swear silently to himself.

Grimly he regarded the streaks of red, yellow and gold mingling on the center of the table. "Hand 'em over." *Before your mother sees this.*

"No! We do it ourselves!" the trio chanted in unison, rising up on their knees and clutching their bottles even more tightly. Unfortunately, though they initially aimed down at their plates, the force they put into squeezing the bottles pushed the bottoms of the containers down, toward themselves, and the tops up—straight at him. Before he could do more than take a breath, a spray of red splashed across his nicely ironed shirt. Another messy arc of yellow followed. The plastic honey bear squirted sticky goo.

And that was, of course, the moment Rose chose to walk back in.

Clint looked at her.

But she was staring pointedly at her children.

Abruptly chastened, the triplets sat back down, evidently prepared to use perfect manners now that their mom was back.

"Really?" She put her hands on her hips and asked sternly, "Is this how we treat our guests?"

All eyes lowered. "Sorry," the three mumbled.

Their apology accepted, Rose collected the condiment bottles and took them over to the sink. She deposited the sticky mess with a sigh. "Kids, please eat your dinner."

Pretty chin set, she pivoted and crooked an authoritative finger at Clint. Clearly she was not about to let him off the hook anywhere near as easily.

"While you," she said, locking eyes with him, "come with me."

Chapter Three

Rose led the way to the only semiprivate area on the bungalow's first floor—the foyer.

Once there, she pivoted so the hand-carved staircase was against her spine and folded her arms in front of her. "So much for leaving a cowboy in charge."

Clint tried not to notice how the fading sunlight pouring in through the transom over the door illuminated the golden highlights in her dark-blond hair. "Hey, I can wrangle a kiddo or two. I just wasn't expecting that."

"Noted," Rose said dryly. "And for the record, you're going to want to put some water on those stains as soon as possible—otherwise that handsome shirt of yours will be permanently ruined."

Clint looked down at the splashes of ketchup, mustard and honey marring the otherwise pristine white-and-blue tattersall-plaid shirt. He shrugged. "Wouldn't be the first time."

"Yeah, but this calamity was due to my kids, so…" Her voice trailing off, Rose looked him up and down, shaking her head in mute consternation. "You know, the stains aren't just here." She made a sweeping gesture, her glance moving down past his throat, to the center of his chest, to his waist, back up along his sleeves. "You've even got some in your hair and on your cheek." She motioned to a place just next to his ear.

However, Clint couldn't help but note, the flour on her face was gone.

One of the other ladies must have told her.

Which was a shame. He would have liked to have seen to that himself.

She winced, oblivious to the licentious direction of his thoughts. "Seriously, I'm sorry you got caught in the middle of the triplets' never-ending quest for culinary independence."

"And here I thought it was just the prelude to a preschool-style food fight."

"I wish," she replied ruefully. "Anyway, again, my apologies…"

It didn't escape his attention that the first two buttons on her blouse were undone, revealing a triangle of creamy, soft skin above her breasts. Ignoring the pressure building behind his fly, Clint smiled back. "I think I'll survive."

She laughed. "I imagine you will."

Their gazes locked. Something changed in her eyes, a flicker of vulnerability glimmering in their beautiful green depths. His pulse amped up as she drew another quick breath.

"But in the meantime, I insist you do something about that shirt before it's ruined." She gestured toward the second floor. "The bathrooms are upstairs. Fresh linens—and the stain remover pens and spray—are in the linen closet in my bathroom. Feel free to help yourself while I return to oversee the minions."

Clint nodded. "Thanks."

He found the higher floor even smaller than the first floor. There were only two bedrooms. One decorated in primary colors sported three youth beds, arranged dormitory-style, with built-in drawers beneath. The bedroom was connected to a small bath, also adorned in bright colors. Monogrammed towels hung from a rack. The bathtub was outfitted with toys and antislip safety decals. A sink with a child-size stepstool in front of it was smudged with toothpaste and hand soap.

He moved on down the hall to the other bedroom, which was obviously Rose's. It held a big four-poster bed with canopy, a padded bench and an old-fashioned makeup table with mirror. Clothes were strewn everywhere, from the closet floor to the end of the unmade bed and the back of an oversize satin chaise, which looked as if it served as a reading chair.

The master bathroom was beyond that, and the only way to get to it—and the linen closet where the stain removal supplies were kept—was to go through the perfume-scented domain.

Telling himself it was no big deal—if it had been, Rose wouldn't have sent him up there—Clint made his way through the softly carpeted lair into the master bathroom.

It, too, was unutterably feminine. Decorated in pink and white. There was a single sink sunk into a wide white cabinet with plenty of drawers. The gray-and-white marble countertop held a variety of hair products, perfumes, makeup, fragrant bubble baths and candles. A big clawfoot soaking tub, outfitted with a showerhead and a circular shower curtain, sat beneath the only window.

A book stand next to the tub overflowed with novels and magazines. More clothes were tossed onto the floor, and a bundle of frilly lingerie spilled out of the hamper.

Standing there, he became aware of two things.

First, Rose was a lot more girlie than he had ever imagined.

And second, there weren't enough hours in the day for her to do everything she needed to accomplish.

And care for her three very active kids.

Which explained the harried look on her face when she answered the door, as well as her penchant for going full steam ahead toward her goal, no matter what the obstacles…

The woman did not have time to mess around.

So she didn't.

He admired her for that—even as the man in him longed to help her out.

"Clint?" A soft voice jerked him from his reverie. "What are you doing?"

He pivoted to see Rose standing in the doorway. Every thought except the possibility of making love with her went out of his brain. Aware she was waiting for some explanation, he finally admitted, "I'm still trying to figure out where the linen closet is."

"Oh. Sorry!" Her cheeks lit with embarrassment as she swooped down to collect her clothes and then stuffed them on top of the lingerie. "I forgot about this mess when I sent you up here—"

He stopped her with a hand on her arm and drew her around to face him. He wanted her to know that as far as her personal life was concerned, he had nothing but admiration for her. "That's not what distracted me."

Struggling to get her balance, she glanced up at him in bewilderment. "Then what did?"

Clint tightened his grip to steady her. The feel of her body beneath his fingers sent a fresh wave of desire roaring through him. All thoughts of being a gentleman fled. He pulled her against him and did what he'd been wanting to do for days now. "This."

ROSE HAD SWORN never again to be reckless when it came to her love life. Now she was conscientious and responsible to a fault. But something about this man brought out the passionate side of her.

Something that made her want him as badly as he seemed to want her. "Clint..." she murmured, splaying her hands across his broad chest. She felt the strong, steady beat of his heart beneath her fingertips. Saw his head lower, his eyes shut. And then there was no more thinking, no more talking, only the masterful sensation of his lips moving over hers and the erotic sweep of his tongue.

He tasted like mint. He kissed like a man who always got what he wanted. And what he wanted right now, Rose realized as his muscular frame pressed her achingly close, was her.

The trouble was, she wanted him, too. Had from the first moment they had squared off alone, under the hot Texas sun, days before.

She didn't know what it was about him, she thought as he cupped her face in his hands and ever-so-slowly deepened the kiss. The fact that he was incredibly straightforward? She'd never have to worry about him hiding what was on his mind, because he was the kind of guy who would just flat-out tell her. Or was it her sense that he could see things about her no one else did? Or the oft-guarded look in his eyes that said he had suffered his share of life's hurts and disappointments in their years apart, too?

All Rose knew for certain was that with just one kiss, he had her surrendering to the warm, sure pressure of his mouth in a way she never had before.

And that could not be, she knew.

Not with her three children right downstairs.

CLINT WASN'T SURPRISED when Rose tore her mouth from his and pushed him away. Hard.

The kiss had been completely unwarranted, given the situation. Yet he couldn't say he was sorry he had done it. Because it had made at least one thing very clear: the two of them had the kind of attraction that was not to be denied.

Not if he had anything to do with it, anyway.

Her breath coming in unsteady puffs, she stepped back and shot him an indignant glare.

"Sorry about that," he said more or less automatically, regaining his manners.

She harrumphed and narrowed her pretty eyes. "*Are* you?"

He chuckled. So she wanted him to be blunt? "Of course not." *Any more than you are.*

Her scowl deepened in a way that made him want to haul her into his arms and kiss her all over again. "Then?"

He rubbed his jaw with the back of his hand, considering. Eventually he decided to go with the truth. "Seemed like the polite thing to say, given the way you just kissed me back. And maybe wish you hadn't?"

Rose sighed, unable to mask completely the turbulent emotion on her face. "With good reason." She shoved a hand through her unruly curls, pushing the silky strands away from her forehead. "Unlike you, it's not just me I have to worry about."

Aware she had a point, Clint sobered. "Where are the triplets?"

"They're downstairs, drawing you some 'I'm Sorry for Making a Mess on Your Shirt' pictures for you to take home."

Reminded of why he had ventured up there in the first place, Clint looked at her formerly all-peach blouse. "Speaking of messes..." he drawled, pointing to her left breast.

She glanced down, saw the smear of honey, ketchup and mustard that spread from heart to sternum and looked even more horrified.

Knowing the tension needed to be eased, Clint quipped, "Well, at least you got some of it off my clothes. Although maybe not in the way we intended."

IF SHE HAD been the kind of gal to throw a punch, she really would have decked the sexy cowboy opposite her right about now. For kissing her and making her feel the kinds of things she most certainly did not want to feel. Fortunately for both of them, she had always been able to keep her temper under wraps.

"Cute." Rose brushed by him, headed for the linen closet. To get to it, she had to tug aside the circular shower curtain, which had been gathered in front of it.

Her back to Clint, she eased the closet door open and brought out a spray bottle of stain remover, several cleaning and pretreating pens, a washcloth and a towel.

Swinging back around, she gasped.

"Now what?" he asked, appearing even more baffled.

Rose's eyes widened in shock. She'd thought he had been sexy as could be when he'd been all sweaty and working on the tractor. That was *nothing* compared with how magnificent he looked when freshly showered and shaven, smelling of leather and spice. "You took your shirt off!"

He gestured aimlessly, more comfortable half-naked than she could ever hope to be.

"What was I supposed to do? I can't have it on while you spray the stains." Furrowing his brow, he nodded at the green bottle in her hand. "I'm allergic to that stuff."

"Why didn't you tell me that?"

He lounged against her bathroom counter, legs crossed at the ankle, arms folded across his brawny chest. "Wasn't worth arguing about. Besides," he teased, "it's not like you haven't seen me with my shirt off before. Monday—"

She cut him off with an indignant huff. "I remember." Boy, did she ever remember. She'd dreamed about it two nights in a row. Only in her dreams, his shirt wasn't all he had taken off.

Meanwhile, he evidently had his own unshared thoughts. His gaze drifted over her lazily, lingering on the stains—

which happened to be mostly across her breasts—before leisurely cataloguing her throat and face, and returning to linger, even more seductively, on her eyes. "Then what's the big deal?" he asked huskily.

The big deal was they'd just been making out, Rose thought in exasperation. *The big deal* was his nipples were still every bit as taut as hers. Not that she had needed that confirmation. His strong arousal had been evident elsewhere, too...

Rose shut her eyes for a moment, willing the desire welling inside her to go away. Then she asked with exaggerated patience, "Do you have any other shirts with you? In your truck, maybe?" A lot of people who worked outdoors—like herself—carried extra.

He continued watching her, inscrutable now. "No."

She did her best to become poker-faced as well. "Are you interested in a Rose Hill Farm T-shirt?"

"Sure. Except it would have to be washed first. Because I'm allergic to a lot of the anti-wrinkle coatings on new clothes, too."

Aware she no longer needed the stain removers, at least in that moment, she set them down. "You really are difficult."

Clint shrugged his shirt back on. Winked. "And in other respects, I am apparently oh-so-easy."

Not from what she had heard.

He hadn't dated anyone since he had been back in town. In fact, he had been as monk-like in his life as she had been nun-like in hers. At least, she'd been nun-like up until the last month or so.

Which begged the question—why had he kissed her?

Why was he still looking like he wanted to put the moves on her again? And most importantly, why did she want him to do just that?

Rose swallowed and tried to pull herself together.

"Look," he said. "All kidding aside, there's no reason for you to worry about my shirt. I'll just take it home and wash it there in the detergent I know I'm not allergic to."

Like he had originally suggested.

Sighing, Rose watched him button his stained shirt from the bottom. She'd let pure passion lead her astray once before and knew better than to let it happen again, no matter what her still-humming body wanted. "Maybe that would be best."

Together they headed back downstairs. They'd just reached the foyer when the doorbell rang. Rose moaned.

Clint slid a hand beneath her elbow and slanted her a glance. "Not expecting anyone?"

"No. But it's always like this when a brand-new crop of good produce comes in."

Belatedly seeming to realize he still had a grip on her, Clint dropped his hand and peered at the clock—which now said seven-thirty. From the kitchen, the kids could be heard chattering about their drawings. "Don't you have regular business hours?"

"Yes," Rose said, over her shoulder, opening the door, "And no."

On the other side stood her triplet sisters, Violet and Lily. And the oldest of them all only single-birth Mc-Cabe daughter, Poppy.

The trio took in Rose's shirt, then Clint's. In unison, they started to laugh. Then Poppy blurted out, "What have you two been up to?"

Chapter Four

Rose was trying to figure out how to answer that when the triplets joined them, artwork in hand.

"Hi, aunts," they said.

"Hi, kids," Poppy, Lily and Violet said in return, setting down a picnic basket and zip-style insulated nylon cooler.

"We got in trouble," Scarlet announced, pushing her glasses up higher on her nose.

Stephen nodded. "For getting stuff all over Mr. Clint's nice shirt."

"And your mom's," Violet added helpfully, looking as tired as usual after one of her oncology residency shifts at Laramie Community Hospital.

Sophia's brow creased.

Uh-oh, Rose thought. *Here comes trouble.*

"We didn't get any stuff on Mommy," Sophia declared.

All three kids looked at Rose's shirt in bewilderment.

"Mommy!" Stephen shrieked, "How did you *do* that?"

Lily—who was now happily married, with a baby on the way—glanced from Rose to Clint. "I think I know," she teased.

So, apparently, did Violet and Poppy. Neither of whom were known for keeping their opinions regarding romance to themselves.

Doing her best to hang on to her composure, which

wasn't easy given how the more deeply imprinted stains on Clint's shirt matched up with the lighter ones on hers, Rose purposely dodged the question. "The point is," she continued, looking straight at her offspring, "Sophia, Scarlet and Stephen know how to use their table manners and not make a mess of our guests."

Apparently unable to resist, Poppy ribbed her, "Do the grown-ups know it, too?"

Luckily the joke went over the triplets' heads. Not so Clint's, who was standing there with a choirboy innocence definitely not to be believed.

Not sure how the situation could get any more embarrassing unless they'd actually been caught in flagrante, Rose cleared her throat. *Definitely time to steer the subject to safer territory.*

Ignoring the amused twinkle in Clint's eyes that only she could see, she plastered an encouraging smile on her face. "So...do you kids want to show Mr. Clint what you made for him?"

Pride straightened their little spines. "We made 'sorry' pictures!" Sophia declared shyly.

Wordlessly, the triplets handed them over one by one. Stephen had drawn an airplane in the clouds. Sophia had colored her version of a fairy princess. Scarlet had drawn the pet dog she one day hoped to have. They had all printed their names on the bottom, just as they had learned to do in their Montessori preschool.

Clint studied the awkward-looking letters beneath the heartfelt drawings and the earnest expressions on the children's upturned faces. "Well, thank you, kids," he said, his voice suddenly sounding a little rusty.

"You're welcome," the triplets said happily in unison, relieved to have gotten themselves out of trouble. Again.

Rose glanced at her watch. "It's almost time for baths,

but you have ten minutes, if you want to go outside and play on the swing set."

"Okay, Mommy!" With yells of delight, they raced off.

The adults exchanged glances rife with even more questions. Not about to have another inquiry start, Rose took the handsome cowboy by the elbow. She half expected him to resist her direction. Instead, he leaned into her touch, much the same way he had when he'd been kissing her.

A tingle went through her palm. Another welled in her middle. Ignoring both, Rose lifted her chin stubbornly. "Clint was just leaving…" she said.

Her sisters looked contrite.

"Listen, we had no idea the two of you were dating," Lily said quickly, running a hand through her honey-blond hair. "Otherwise we wouldn't have just barged in."

"That's for sure. And he's a lot better than some of the other duds you have spent time with recently," Poppy put in cheerfully, one hand resting on the laptop bag looped over her slender shoulder.

Clint quirked a brow. "Thanks. I think."

Rose shot him a look that said, *Please don't encourage them!* She turned back to her sisters. "We're not dating."

Unexpectedly, Clint draped an arm across her shoulders. "We could be," he said with a wicked smile.

Ignoring the amusement on her sisters' faces, Rose removed his arm. Stepped to one side. Looked up at him with a warning glance. "I don't think so."

"Why not?" he drawled.

Rose ignored the sexual heat in his sable-brown eyes. "You wouldn't have to ask that if you'd ever been married."

Hooking his thumbs through his belt loops, he rocked forward on the toes of his boots. Shrugged carelessly. "Actually, I almost was."

She refused to let down her guard. "Almost doesn't count," she retorted.

He tilted his head to one side, thinking, clearly aware he was annoying her terribly. "It does if you're the one who nearly made a life-altering mistake."

"Wow," Poppy said, looking ready to break out the popcorn and take a seat. "It just gets better."

Rose scowled at her oldest sister, who was one to talk since she was the most independent and had never really risked anything in the romance department. "Or worse," she returned dryly, "depending on your point of view."

Clint waved like a highway worker, trying to get her attention. "I'm still hanging in here."

"Not wisely," Rose huffed.

Lily peered at them curiously. Then she continued, using her skills as an attorney turned mayor turned mediator. "So if the two of you aren't dating, and aren't going to date—"

"That's yet to be decided," Clint interrupted mildly, more confident than ever.

Rose drew in a deep breath. And stared at him like he'd grown a second head.

"Well," he said, refusing to back down, "it hasn't been."

"Maybe not by *you*," Rose snapped, temper flaring, reminding herself yet again why she was not going to let herself be distracted by passion, or even the potential of it.

If—and it was a big if—she ever got involved with someone again, it would be because they were perfect for each other in all ways outside the bedroom. Not just in.

"Then why *is* he here?" Violet asked. "And why were you obviously, ah…in his arms…if the two of you, ah, aren't…?"

Aware her sisters were jumping to far too many conclusions and the man opposite her was way too handsome—and distracting—for comfort, Rose rubbed her temples and shut her eyes. "He came over to talk to me."

"About?" Lily pressed.

Good point! Rose sucked in a breath, curious now, too. "I was just about to find out." She opened her eyes again. Put one palm on Clint's back, the other beneath his elbow. Steered the big guy deliberately toward the front door. "So if you, dear sisters, will excuse us…and keep an eye on my kids, to boot…" she said over her shoulder.

"Not to worry," Lily called out merrily. "Take your time!"

Clint chuckled and shut the door behind them, once again leaving the two of them very much alone. "Oh, I plan to," he replied.

THIS TIME, CLINT NOTED, Rose did not even try to stifle her groan.

"You are *not* going to kiss me again," she said, marching him down the sidewalk to his pickup truck.

She sure had a one-track mind.

Not that he hadn't been ruminating over the first time he'd taken her in his arms, too.

Even though he knew darn well it would be asking for trouble.

"Wasn't planning to," he shot back. The enormity of her relief prompted him to add teasingly, "Now."

Soft lips twisting into a pretty glower, Rose adapted a militant stance. "What did you want to see me about?" she asked, folding her arms in front of her.

Trying not to notice the way the action plumped up her breasts, he countered, "Sure you don't want our conversation to wait, with your sisters peering out the windows and all?"

Rose cast a glance over her shoulder. She waved her family away. The blinds closed completely. "I'd rather hear it now." Still he hesitated. "Come on, Clint, spill it. I'm curious."

So much for trying to keep the unexpected feelings of intimacy and cautious goodwill flowing between them.

But since she'd made it abundantly clear that she was not going to drop it, Clint figured he might as well bite the bullet. So he sobered. Straightened. And adapted his own semi-militant stance. "Well, if you must know," he muttered, "I did not appreciate the dozen women you sent out to help me this morning. Again, without warning."

It took her a moment to understand what he was talking about. "Oh, the co-op moms!"

A group of women who had never stopped talking—to each other and, unfortunately, to him. Thereby eradicating his dream of long days spent outdoors amid peace and quiet. "I didn't need their help."

"Oh, really." The sass was back in her eyes, reeling him back in. "And how long would it have taken you today to get a truckload of berries without their assistance?"

He wouldn't have achieved that at all. Not in one day. He clenched his jaw. "That's not the point."

She hovered closer, surrounding him with a drift of citrus on a sunny day. "It's exactly the point, cowboy. Blackberries are very perishable once they are picked. They need to be refrigerated quickly. Having co-op members come over to your ranch and help get them onto the refrigerator truck goes a long way to preserving the fruit's great taste and longevity."

Clint shoved a hand through his hair, aware that, as usual, he needed a haircut. "As I told you before...I can't afford to pay anyone to assist with the harvest."

"You don't have to. The co-op members—many of whom are male, by the way—work for points that enable them to purchase produce at a very steep discount. Because they physically help with the harvest, they also get first dibs on anything that comes in."

Turning, she walked over to his pickup truck and waited

for him to follow. "The rest of the produce goes to Rose Hill Farm clients. Grocery stores, farm stands, small mom-and-pop markets and restaurant chefs."

He wasn't surprised to discover she ran two businesses. One that helped the community, the other her own bottom line. That did not mean, however, that he was all right with the onslaught.

He moved nearer despite himself. Aware he was wanting to kiss her again, badly, he fished in his pocket for his keys. "I can't have a dozen women out there underfoot every day."

She nodded, understanding. "You won't. Today was just a day to get the feel of how this is all going to work. From now on, you'll only have two co-op members there at a time. And only during school hours."

He propped a shoulder against the truck and released a breath, his tension easing a bit.

"So if you get started earlier or go later—" Rose continued.

"I'll have the peace and quiet I want?" he interrupted with a grin.

The peace that had seemed ideal until he'd spent a half an hour in her home and become aware all over again of everything he wanted and was missing. Kids. A wife. Happy family chaos.

She rolled her eyes. "Your wish is my command, cowboy."

Another spark lit between them.

Rose stepped in the direction of the house, abruptly becoming wary again. "Well, I've got to get back to my sisters…"

On impulse, he caught her wrist and rubbed the inside of it with his thumb. Then felt her tremble, just as she had when he'd held her in his arms.

He was tempted to ask her out, but knew this was the

wrong time and the wrong place, unless he wanted to be spurned again.

"Are they going to give you the business?" he murmured softly instead.

She sighed. "Probably."

BECAUSE SHE HAD her siblings' help, Rose was able to get the three kids bathed and tucked into bed in record time. Finished, she went back down to the kitchen, where she soon discovered her dishes had been done, too. A more adult repast was laid out. They'd obviously brought it with them.

Sisters. Rose heaved a contented sigh, sitting down at the table with them. *What would she do without them?*

She hoped never to find out.

Violet cut into the warm, puff pastry–wrapped brie.

Poppy passed around crisp green apple and pear slices. "We all had heard you'd sweet-talked Clint McCulloch into harvesting the Double Creek Ranch blackberry crop. But we had no idea he'd been pursuing you."

No kidding.

Not wanting to admit how recently that had started, never mind how quickly Clint had turned her whole world upside down—with just one kiss!—Rose adopted her best poker face. "He's not, really."

"Then why were you kissing him?"

Knowing it would be futile to deny they had been making out, just a little, Rose stated cagily, "Impulse. A bad one at that, and one that won't happen again. So…to what do I owe the honor of this visit?"

Poppy raised her glass of sparkling water in toast. "I finally got Trace Caulder to agree to adopt with me!"

Everyone clinked glasses. Rose asked, "But you're not planning to get married to the Lieutenant?"

The thirty-five-year-old Poppy waved off the possibility. "It's not really necessary these days. At least through the private agency we're using."

No one knew better than Rose how hard it could be to raise a family as a single mother. On the other hand, she had all the McCabes behind her, helping out as needed. And so would Poppy, whose interior-design business was based in Laramie.

Poppy tore her hunk of French bread into bite-size pieces. "I'm not cut out to be a military wife. And Trace doesn't want to give up flying jets for the Air Force. But we're best friends—"

And lovers, whenever the good Lieutenant was stateside, Rose thought.

"—and we both want a family, sooner rather than later," Poppy continued, practical as ever. "So this is the best option for both of us. The problem is, the agency wants photos of me and Trace together that exemplify us as potential parents. And the last time we had any taken was at Lily's wedding. Prior to that, it was Callie and Maggie's double wedding."

Though, Rose thought, only one of their older twin sisters had actually gotten married that day.

"We'll all help you look," Violet promised. Although the search was likely to produce an upsetting number of photos of Violet's late fiancé, Sterling, and Rose and her ex-husband, too.

Nevertheless, as soon as their meal was over, Rose put on a pot of coffee. Together, they all went through the pictures.

"None of these are right," Poppy said finally with a defeated sigh.

"Maybe I have something on my computer of the two of you," Rose told her, glad to move away from remnants of her disastrous romantic past, too.

"Why don't we all go through our picture files?" Violet suggested. "And get back to each other when we find more to choose from."

Anything, Rose agreed, to keep her mind off the unexpected turn her own life had taken and the mistake she had recklessly made. She'd had one relationship based on passion—and little else—that had crashed and burned. She wasn't going to embark on another.

"So you do know who Rose has been dating," Clint said to Gannon several days later when the two got together to repair a line of fence that ran between their ranches.

Gannon chuckled and shoved a post-digger into the ground. "The question is, what is it to you?"

Clint shrugged, trying not to think about the fact that Rose had been avoiding him like the plague, not coming out to his ranch once since he'd kissed her. Nor had she been the one driving the refrigerated truck back and forth from Rose Hill Farm. She had Swifty doing that for her. And for reasons he couldn't quite fathom, her absence really irked him, knowing he was on her Out List. Just for making his intention of pursuing her clear.

He set a new wooden post into the foot-deep hole, packed it tight with the displaced dirt, then turned to his happily married friend. "Let's just say I don't want to unwittingly repeat some other dude's mistakes."

"I wouldn't, either, if I were you." Gannon moved on down the line to the next post in need of replacement. Using a crowbar and shovel, he worked it out of the dirt. "Although I don't know what precisely those missteps were."

The way cleared, Clint used both hands to center a new wooden post squarely in the hole.

"Just that she dumped him?" Clint asked.

"Them," Gannon corrected.

"There's been more than one?" Clint blinked in surprise.

Gannon paused to wipe the sweat from his brow with one gloved hand. "Three or four, at least. But she dumped every one of them after one date."

Not much of a chance to succeed or impress.

"Any idea why?"

Gannon cut a strip of barbed wire from another weak post. "That you would have to ask her. Maybe the next time you're putting the moves on her, you could bring it up." He dropped the wire into the bed of the pickup truck with the rest of the metal, then added with a smirk, "I heard about the condiments on the shirts. Smooth."

Clint winced. Were he and Rose *ever* going to live that down? It seemed the twins had mentioned that incident to everyone in their preschool, who in turn had gone home and told their parents. Hence, a lot of the co-op moms had joked about it when they'd come out to work on the Double Creek blackberry patch harvest.

Muttering under his breath, Clint took a turn with the digger. "You think Rose is mad at me about that?"

"Only one way to find out," Gannon drawled.

Clint nodded his understanding. "I'm going to have to ask her."

Chapter Five

Clint did not like being counted out before he'd even begun. He also didn't like the way he had been wondering about Rose McCabe. The way she and her rambunctious trio of kids always seemed to be on his mind now.

And there was only one cure for that, he knew. Remove the aura of mystery. Bring her—and the sparks they always seemed to generate—squarely into reality.

So Saturday afternoon, when the day's bounty was in, he drove the co-op truck to Rose Hill Farm, around to the loading dock in the back.

Rose walked out to greet him. Except for the fringe of bangs across her forehead, her hair was drawn up in a clip on the back of her head. She was wearing jeans and a long-sleeved co-op T-shirt with the sleeves pushed halfway up her forearms. Her soft lips were bare of lipstick, and the color of exertion stained her cheeks. Although there was still a lot of energy in her movements, she looked a little tired around the eyes.

And not at all pleased to see him.

"Where's Swifty?" she bit out.

Wishing she weren't so deliciously disheveled, Clint cut the motor and hopped down from the cab. "He had a barbecue to go to this evening. I told him I'd do the honors."

"You realize that means unloading the crates, too?"

Pushing aside the desire to kiss her, he opened the rear doors of the refrigerated truck. "Just show me where to put them."

Wordlessly she turned on her heel, then stalked back into the barn, returning with a long wheeled cart similar to the luggage caddies used in hotels.

As eager to get business concluded as she was so he could take things to a more personal level, Clint worked silently at her side. Together they were able to stack nine crates on the six-foot stainless-steel tray, then move it through the open barn doors and into an adjacent refrigeration room that seemed to comprise most of the barn.

Inside was a bounty of other fresh-picked vegetables and fruits. Rose showed him where to stack the berries, then grabbed a second cart for herself. They shut the door and went back to the truck.

Unloading took half an hour of repeated trips back and forth. Finally they were finished. Clint helped her close up and lock the back of the truck, then followed her out of the refrigeration room to sign off on the day's delivery invoices. As they moved through the high-ceilinged, cement-floored building, he shortened his stride to match hers.

"Where are your kids?" he asked, all too aware of how good she smelled. Like soap and the citrusy fragrance she favored.

"With my family."

He tracked the loose strands of hair escaping from her clip and grazing the elegant nape of her neck.

Oblivious to the growing pressure at the front of his jeans, Rose led the way past the display area to a glass-walled office with her name on the door, then stepped inside.

Using the figures she'd typed into her phone, she sank down into the chair behind her desk and completed an invoice. Rising, she met his eyes and handed it to him to sign, too. Their hands brushed in the process. Once again he was surprised at how soft and feminine and delicate her skin felt.

She met his gaze with a rueful grin. "Saturday is always a tough day for me. A lot of co-op members come by to pick up their weekly orders."

Clint checked the invoice over and then scribbled his name. She tore off his copy, handed his over and put the rest on the inbox on her desk. He folded his up and slid it into the chest pocket of his shirt. "But you're done now."

She nodded. "I close at four."

Which had been nearly an hour ago. Hence the building appeared deserted except for the two of them. Not surprised she was the last on the scene and probably the first to arrive, too, Clint walked with her back out of her office, past a line of checkout registers.

Glad she seemed in no hurry to show him the door now that the work was done, he looked around in awe. "This is…"

"Not what you expected?" she interrupted with a triumphant smile.

"I was going to say very modern." He gestured at the bank of computers and phones. "And a lot more high-tech than I would have imagined."

She walked over to a small break area. Denim stretched over her very fine derriere as she bent to look inside the glass-front cooler. Pulling out two bottles of flavored water, she straightened and tossed him one.

Ignoring his immediate physical reaction to the succulent sight of her, he accepted the drink with a smile. "Thanks." Resolved to think about something else, lest he be tempted to put the moves on her again, he inclined his head at the blackboard across one wall. It was filled with the names of local farms and the dates of the crops currently coming in. "Are these all your suppliers?"

Rose sank down into a swivel chair and propped her feet up on the seat of another. "Yep. Although there's always room for more."

He studied her fancy red cowgirl boots with a scrolling of roses and thorns up the sides. Which was pretty much a perfect depiction of the woman wearing them. Incredibly feisty and feminine, if you could get past the thorns. He settled in a chair opposite her and returned his attention to her face, trying not to notice all over again just how beautiful she was.

"How did you get into this?" Savoring his rare time alone with her, he uncapped his bottle and drank deeply of the pomegranate-flavored water. "Last I heard, you were a pharmaceutical sales rep."

"I was." Wincing, Rose pulled the clip from her hair. "Until the triplets were born and my husband and I divorced."

He watched as she ran her fingers over her scalp, freeing and loosening the cloud of silky curls, then let her hand fall back to her lap. "When was that?" he asked.

"We separated a few months after I gave birth. The actual divorce came through when the triplets were one year old."

She seemed to have handled the split well, yet empathy stirred inside him nonetheless. "That must have been tough."

"Aren't all divorces?" Though the corners of her luscious lips turned downward, she pushed on with her story. "But thankfully, since Barry surrendered all his parental rights and took a job elsewhere, at least I didn't have a custody battle on my hands."

"Your ex was a damn fool," Clint said gruffly. "Giving up you and those kids."

Rose flashed a wan smile and met his eyes, reluctantly

accepting his sympathy. "After that, I decided to leave Dallas and return to Laramie."

"To be near your family," he guessed, his heart going out to her all over again. He'd had his own disappointments. But nothing as traumatic as what she'd been through.

She nodded. "Obviously I couldn't work outside the home at that point—and simultaneously give three infants the tender loving care they needed—so I reluctantly moved back in with my parents for a while, and paid our expenses with what was left of my savings and the child support Barry had been ordered to pay.

"As you can imagine, money was tight, but I still wanted to feed the kids well. So I started calling around to some of the farmers in the area, asking if I could bypass the wholesalers and middlemen and buy straight from them. Other people I knew asked me to do the same for them, which I did—for an upcharge."

Smart, he thought, not really surprised, given that he'd never met a more energetic or enterprising woman than the one sitting next to him.

"About that time the whole Buy Local movement took off, so with the help of a loan from my parents, I purchased this property, rechristened it Rose Hill Farm and set up shop here. From there, it made sense to add a co-op to my already existing wholesale business." Rose drew a breath that lifted and lowered the shapely lines of her soft breasts.

A jolt of pure heat went through him. Clint shifted in his chair, tempted to push the limits with her once again. "It's bloomed into quite a business."

"And not just in Laramie County." Rose stood and strode over to throw her empty bottle in the recycling bin. "I've even started supplying the upscale Fresh Foods Markets in Dallas on a limited crop-by-crop basis, which benefits everyone."

Finally seeing a way to steer the conversation where he wanted it, he stood, too.

"Even the guys you've been dating?" Clint asked, determined to find out who his competition had been. And more importantly, just why they had failed to win a pivotal place in her life. He didn't want to make the same mistake.

DECIDING SHE'D SPENT far too much time alone with the handsome cowboy, Rose fished the keys off her belt and headed for the barn entrance.

As expected, Clint was right behind her. "Why do you care?" She threw the words over her shoulder.

He overtook her at the doorway and stepped out into the dwindling spring sunshine. Thanks to daylight saving time, it wouldn't get dark for another two hours, but the skies were still a clear blue and the temperature—which had been in the high eighties all day—was now dropping. Which meant a very pleasant star-filled evening ahead.

She locked up. "I didn't think you were into gossip."

He lounged casually beside her, one brawny shoulder propped against the red siding. "Call me curious."

Wondering how in the heck he could still look so darn good after being out in the field all day, she shot back, "Well, don't be." With five sisters and two parents prying into her love life, or lack thereof, she didn't need any more questions.

He ignored her subtle gibe and pressed closer. Determined, it seemed, to know everything about her. Even as she vowed to continue to keep him at arm's length.

"Then they were guys you're involved with in a business sense."

"No. Not at all." Rose pivoted and began strolling across the yard, toward her bungalow. "One was a cardiologist. Another a computer programmer. The third an insurance agent."

He fell into step beside her. "So what happened?"

Resisting the crazy urge to tuck her hand into his, she kept on going. "None of them could handle the kids—even during the thirty-minute predate get-to-know-each-other sessions. And the triplets didn't like the guys, either." Rose sighed as she mounted the steps to the front door of her house. "And that clearly wasn't likely to change."

"So you quit dating."

As if it had been that simple! Figuring the only way to get him to back off was to lay it all on the line, Rose spun toward him. "Do you know what the divorce rate of parents of multiples is right now?"

He shook his head.

Unsure whether it was resentment or nerves prodding her to respond so emotionally, Rose told him the stark awful truth. "Over 70 percent."

"Well, that's discouraging."

Tell me about it!

Deciding not to go into the house after all, Rose went back to the wide steps leading up to her front porch and sat down. "If I couldn't make it work with the biological father of my children, what are my odds of making something work with a guy who has no connection to them?"

He shrugged and sat down next to her. "Depends on the guy."

Her heartbeat quickened at the unexpected compassion in his low tone. She thought about the kisses they had already shared, and how quickly he had rocked her world. "I suppose you'd be up for the challenge?" she queried dryly.

An affable grin deepened the crinkles around his eyes. "Damn straight I would."

She shook her head. Sighed.

"You don't believe me?" he asked, cocky.

Rose stood once again, eager now to have him on his way. "I believe you want to think you could handle what no other man has. But reality is quite another thing. And the bottom line is," she said, lifting her chin, "I don't want my kids getting hurt."

He got to his feet, too, his dark gaze skimming her intently. "Keep telling yourself that. You're guaranteed to be miserable."

Finding his low, rumbling voice a bit too determined—and too full of sexual promise—for comfort, she returned, "Excuse me?"

Folding his arms in front of him, he braced his legs a little farther apart. "You're not afraid for your kids," he stated with a smug smile. "You're afraid for you."

"I am not."

He strolled toward her. "Then prove it," he said, looking very much like he wanted to make love with her right then and there. "And go out with me."

Knowing it would be a dangerous proposition to have him that close to her—because she did desire him more than anyone who had ever come before—Rose shook her head. "That would never work."

His expression guarded, he studied her. "Why not?"

Feeling hot color flush her cheeks, Rose enunciated as clearly as possible, "Because we have absolutely nothing in common."

He took her in his arms, reassuring her with a wink. His mouth hovered over hers. "We have this."

Rose had been telling herself she had imagined the impact of their first kiss. That it had been the surprise—coupled with the lack of romance in her life—that had left her reeling and wanting more. Even though she knew how very unwise that was.

But now, with his lips seducing hers apart and his tongue tangling with hers, she couldn't help but explore whatever this was turning out to be, at least a little more. She went up on tiptoe, wreathing her arms about his wide shoulders, even as he clasped her closer. Her breasts molded to the hardness of his chest. His arms wrapped around her middle, lifting her until their hearts beat in tandem. Lower still, there was a building pressure and a tingling that stole her breath.

He wanted her. Fiercely. And she reveled in the strength of that demand. Yet she was smart enough to realize that if she let the reckless embrace continue, there would be nothing but heartache and regret for both of them.

And she couldn't have that. Hadn't she already been hurt enough by her ex? Wasn't she still paying for the ramifications of a relationship based solely on passion and little else?

Furious that he'd seduced her into allowing herself to be so vulnerable—again—Rose pushed against Clint's hard, muscular chest and tore her lips away.

Reluctantly, he let her go.

Struggling to regain her equilibrium, she took a step back and dragged in a shaky breath. "I'm not going to date you, Clint."

Skepticism mingled with the impatience on his handsome face. "Why not?" he asked gruffly.

Ignoring the way he was studying her, she declared hoarsely, "Because I'm not available in the way a guy wants me to be."

His gaze roved her upturned face before returning to her eyes. "So you're content to be alone?"

Clearly, Rose noted, he did not believe it.

"I have plenty of companionship, Clint." With three children, five sisters, two parents and dozens of relatives, not to mention friends and business acquaintances in Laramie County, she was always surrounded by people.

He came closer once again, dimples appearing on either side of his wide smile. "What about sex? And romance," he chided softly. "Don't you want that?"

His low, husky murmur sent another waft of desire rippling through her. Blood roared through her veins. Yet nothing of import changed.

The situation still was what it was.

Rose swallowed to ease her parched throat. "It doesn't matter what I want, Clint," she said, trying to ignore the gleam of stark male interest in his eyes. "It matters what I can have. And that's my kids and my business and nothing else." Her brief foray into dating had shown her that.

His expression turned calm, inscrutable. "Just two questions. How long have you been telling yourself this? And how much do you actually believe it?"

As CLINT FIGURED, Rose had no answer for that. Thankfully, for her sake anyway, she was saved from having to answer him by the minivan heading up the drive. It had the McCabe Interiors logo on the side. Poppy was driving, and Rose's three kids waved from their safety seats.

Seeing them, Clint couldn't help but grin.

He had always wanted kids. A wife. A family. Even before the auto accident that claimed his parents' lives and prompted his four sisters to leave the past behind, and seek their fortunes elsewhere. Now that he was back on the Double Creek, missing the family togetherness of his childhood, that yearning had intensified.

"Hey, Mr. Clint!" the three kids yelled as soon as they were out of the vehicle. All three bounded up the porch steps.

Clint offered high-fives, which they all spiritedly returned.

"How are you-all doing?" he asked.

"Good," they crowed in unison.

Clint turned to their aunt. "Hi, Poppy."

"Hello, yourself." She winked as if reading something

into his presence that her sister would have preferred she not. "I hope I'm not interrupting anything…"

Rose gave Poppy a look that said, *Knock it off.* "Business as usual," she replied in a tight, clipped tone.

Clint wished it were. Because that would mean he'd be giving her a helping hand, pleasantly whiling away the time and kissing her every day…

But that wasn't going to be happening if the cantankerous lift of Rose's eyebrow in Poppy's direction was any indication.

Poppy chuckled again, then quickly brought Rose up to speed. "The triplets had lunch around one o'clock. I wish I could tell you that they ate their vegetables, but…"

Scarlet pushed her glasses up on her nose. "We didn't mean to be rude, Mommy!"

"But she put carrots and squash and z'chini in the very same bowl!" Stephen made a face that showed how unappetizing he thought that was.

Sophia momentarily forgot her shyness long enough to chime in, "You know we can't eat food that is *touching*!"

Rose interrupted the diatribe with a stern look. "First of all, is this the way we behave when we are guests in someone else's home?"

Sheepish looks were exchanged all around. Three toes pushed simultaneously into the wood beneath their feet. "No."

Rose chided, "What do you say to your Aunt Poppy?"

Contrite now, the triplets said, "We're sorry." They followed up their words with heartfelt hugs while Rose mouthed "sorry" to her sister, too.

"They already made me their apology pictures," Poppy said. "Which are pictures of veggies, currently hanging on my fridge."

The adults tried not to grin at the irony of that.

"Well, that's good to know," Rose said, pleased, as she

made prolonged eye contact with each one of her children. "Now can you all thank your Aunt Poppy and then go inside and play with your toys 'til dinner?"

An appreciative chorus followed. "Just don't make too big a mess," Rose called after them as the trio raced into the house, already chattering excitedly.

"How's the berry picking going?" Poppy asked Clint casually.

"Better than expected," he admitted.

Thanks to Rose's machinations and the profit he stood to make over the next few weeks, the Double Creek would be a fully operational horse and cattle farm by fall.

Poppy looked at Rose. "Any chance I could get a few blackberries to take home with me?"

Delighted as always to be talking about produce, Rose asked, "Do you want today's crop or part of what I've got in my fridge?"

"The ones inside." Poppy stepped up onto the porch. "Got any of that blackberry cobbler you made last night?"

"Not to worry. There's a piece saved just for you." Rose turned to Clint, as well-mannered as ever. "What about you? Would you like a piece of cobbler to take home with you?"

He never turned down dessert. Plus, from what he had seen so far, anything Rose cooked was bound to be spectacularly good.

Clint tipped the brim of his hat in her direction. "I'd be honored to have some, ma'am."

Poppy laughed at his antics.

Rose shook her head and rolled her eyes. She gestured for them to go first, then followed both her guests inside.

The interior of the house was filled with a wonderful baking smell. In the kitchen, on top of the fridge, sat a glass bowl covered in plastic wrap. It contained a pillowy white dough. For what, exactly, Clint didn't know, but clearly that accounted for the fragrance of homemade goodness in the air.

Rose brought a cobbler out of the fridge and cut two generous slices. As she turned to get two plastic containers out of the cupboard, her T-shirt rode a little higher on her hips, revealing her nice curves beneath her jeans.

He ruminated again on just what it might take to get her where he wanted her. In his arms, in his life, in his bed.

Unaware of the direction of his thoughts, she pivoted back to him. "Just out of curiosity, how do you think this year's crop tastes in comparison to years past?"

Clint shrugged. "I wouldn't know."

"Why?" she asked in surprise. "Because you haven't eaten any in years past?"

"Because I haven't eaten any of them, period."

Rose blinked, as if sure she could not have heard him correctly. Her sister looked equally stunned. He tucked his thumbs in the loops on either side of his belt. "I've been a little busy," he drawled.

Poppy continued to gape. She turned back to Rose, in independent-businesswoman mode now. "How effective of a spokesperson can Clint be if he hasn't even tasted the blackberries from the Double Creek?"

Clint frowned. "I'm selling the harvester, not the crop."

"Hence, in his view, the taste of the berries is irrelevant," Rose said.

But apparently not in hers, Clint noted.

From upstairs, sounds of discord erupted. Poppy picked up her to-go package and answered before Rose could even ask, "Yes. They have been that way all afternoon."

Rose buried her face in her hands as the loud bickering continued. "Now I'm really sorry I asked you to babysit for me all day."

Poppy patted her shoulder. "Don't be. It was a good test to see if I was going to change my mind about wanting kids of my own. Guess what? It didn't. That said, I've got to go." Comically, she pretended to primp. "I'm supposed to Skype with the good Lieutenant later this evening, and I want to do my hair."

Rose chuckled. "Yeah, right."

Clearly, Clint thought, it was an inside joke.

Rose explained, "She never dresses up for Trace."

"The advantage of being just friends." Poppy blew a kiss on her way out the door. "See you!"

Clint knew it was time for him to go, too, especially given the way the triplets were arguing upstairs. Reluctantly he picked up his container of blackberry cobbler, prepared to say goodbye, then was stopped dead in his tracks by an ear-splitting trio of screams.

Chapter Six

Rose stiffened. "What in the world...?"

She raced in the direction of the stairs with Clint hot on her heels. Her pulse pounding, she rounded the corner and swept into the triplets' bedroom. She stopped at what she saw.

The bedcovers were off all three beds.

Toys were scattered here and there.

Most alarming of all, however, was the sight of her three children mid–temper tantrum. She'd thought someone had been seriously hurt—only to discover it was all just a quarrel!

"I'm tired of playing house!" Stephen threw a stuffed animal to the floor. "I want to play soldiers! So I can pretend to be the Lieutenant!"

Poppy, Rose knew, would be pleased to hear that. She'd take it as yet another sign she and her best friend were meant to adopt a baby together.

"We don't want to play soldiers," Scarlet declared, pitching a stack of storybooks.

"Well, I don't want to play only girl stuff!" Stephen added a yell for emphasis and tossed a toy drum.

Sophia, who'd been about to add her two cents to the quarrel despite her shyness, abruptly noticed Rose and Clint in the doorway. "Uh. Oh."

Alerted to impending catastrophe, her siblings stopped mid-rant, spun around, and to Rose's utter relief, finally fell blissfully silent.

"What's the trouble here?" she demanded.

Eager to get their sides heard, all the children spoke at once, confirming what she and Clint had already heard.

"Okay, that's enough." She cut them off with a big referee sweep of both arms. "If you can't think of something to do together—without fighting—you won't be able to play with each other at all. In the meantime, while you are all thinking about that, I want this room straightened up. Pronto. And then you're all having a five-minute time-out."

Clint looked at her, seeming to understand she was near the end of her rope.

"If you want me to stay a while," he whispered, "I will."

Sighing wearily, Rose looked up at him. "Thanks. I'd really appreciate that." It surprised her how much.

HALF AN HOUR LATER, thanks to Clint's steady, reassuring presence, it was a completely different scene.

He had helped Rose and the kids return order to their room, then escorted the youngsters out back for a little outdoor play while Rose got dinner started. Eventually he came in to get some juice boxes for them, then returned to see if he could help her with anything else.

Grateful for all he'd done, she poured him a tall glass of iced tea with mint. Since he seemed in no more hurry to go than he had been earlier, she gestured for him to have a seat on the other side of the kitchen island. "Thanks for kicking around the soccer ball with the kids."

"Happy to do it." He looked out the dining area window at the fenced backyard, where all three kids were now swinging side by side. "They seem to be playing nicely now."

Trying not to notice how right it felt with Clint hanging

out in her kitchen, she said, "Let's hope it continues until I can get dinner ready."

He caught her eye and flashed that easy grin she loved. "What are you making?"

Rose slid last night's oven-roasted veggies into the food processor, added a can of cooked tomatoes, and pulsed until it was smooth and thick. "Pizza sauce."

His gaze slid down the hollow of her throat, past her lips, to her eyes. "With cooked carrots and zucchini?" Or in other words, the very same veggies they'd rejected at Poppy's earlier in the day.

"They'll never know." She added a little salt, pepper and oregano and gave her food processor another whir.

"So. You do this often?"

As always, his ultramasculine presence, the sun-warmed leather scent of him, made her feel protected and intensely aware. Still, in an attempt to regain her equilibrium, she kept her physical distance from him as she dumped the pizza dough onto the cutting board and divided it into eight pieces. "Since they stopped eating vegetables? All the time. Why...you don't approve?"

Taking another long, thirsty drink of iced tea, he watched her roll the dough into thin discs and place them on individual baking rounds. "Not up to me to approve or disapprove."

"But you don't think I should be doing this."

His eyes lit up the way they always did when he knew he'd gotten under her skin. "You want my honest opinion?"

"Yes."

He shrugged and rubbed his palm across his closely shaven jaw, then lazily dropped his hand again. "Doing something underhanded—or covertly—is never a good idea." He squinted in her direction. "It's bound to back-fire on you eventually."

Her temper igniting, she gave him a sharp look. "Says the man with no children of his own."

"So far," he allowed. The tone of his voice implied that might soon change.

The ironic thing was, she could imagine him as a daddy, and a good one. Which of course only made him all the more attractive to her. Pushing her ridiculously romantic notions aside, she forced herself to continue the debate. "Besides, they're not going to find out there's anything in that sauce but tomatoes."

"You *hope* they'll never find out," he scoffed, inclining his head to one side. "The way they're in and out of here…"

He had a point about that. She'd had some near misses. And the last thing she wanted was for her kids to feel she had deliberately misled them in any way.

Clint stood, glass in hand, and strolled back over to the pitcher of tea. He poured more over the ice in his glass and added some to hers, too, then lounged against the counter with his usual ease. "I just think there has to be a better, more direct way."

Rose wasn't sure whether to roll her eyes at his continued naïveté—or laugh. "You really think you could get them to eat veggies again when all other adults have failed?"

The bravura he'd evidenced on the rodeo circuit returned full force. "I do."

"Yeah? Well, I'll bet you can't!"

It was his turn to laugh. "Okay. You're on."

Concluding she really did need to get her head examined for putting herself in such a precarious position, Rose placed her hands on her hips. "So what are the stakes?"

One corner of Clint's lips tilted up in a sexy grin. "I get as much time as I need to make it happen within the span of one week."

Which meant, Rose thought, they'd be seeing each

other—a lot. Another shimmer of tension floated between them, and she felt her breath catch in her throat. Her eyes holding his, she swallowed hard, then stipulated firmly, "However you accomplish it, it has to be out in the open. They have to know they're eating broccoli or whatever. You can't do what you so thoroughly disapprove of me doing and disguise it."

He chuckled, a deep rumbling low in his throat. Then he slowly surveyed her from head to toe as if he found her completely irresistible. "Fair enough."

Trying not to think how attracted she was to him, too, Rose wrinkled her nose. "Now for the winnings…"

Apparently he'd already decided what he wanted. "If I triumph, you go out on a date with me," he drawled.

Rose flushed as she thought about that. A date would mean another kiss, and another kiss would mean…well… "Okay. But if I win," she countered, then stopped to contemplate.

The logical prize would have been the opposite of what he wanted—which was to make him promise never to kiss her again. Oddly enough, she did *not* want that, probably because it was far too predictable a penalty. So she searched her mind for the chore most men complained about this time of year. In a burst of inspiration, she finally said, "You have to mow my lawn!"

He ruminated cheerfully. "Could be sexy."

Especially if he took his shirt off. Rose willed her sudden flash of heat away. Resisting the urge to fan herself, she vowed, "It won't be."

Mischief lit his dark-brown eyes. "Never say never," he taunted her softly.

Was it possible? Were they actually going to end up making love before this was all over?

The back door slammed, saving them both.

"Mommy." The triplets barreled in. "We're hungry!"

Rose directed them over to the kitchen sink. Then she pulled up a stool and supervised the washing of their hands. "Want to help me decorate some individual pizzas?"

They looked adoringly up at their guest, who had come over to wash his hands as well. "Can Mr. Clint make a pizza, too?" Stephen asked.

Rose smiled. "Sure." She looked at Clint, then nodded at the array of colorful toppings she'd put out. "Now's your chance, cowboy." The question was, could he accomplish what she had not?

CLINT SOON REALIZED that Rose had been right. This was not going to be an easy bet to win.

"That sure is a lot of veggies," Stephen said, looking at Clint's creation, which was loaded with peppers, mushrooms and onion as well as crumbles of pepperoni and cooked sausage.

Clint smiled fondly at Rose's son. "I like mine with everything."

Scarlet paused to push her glasses higher on the bridge of her nose. "So does Mommy 'cept she puts olives on hers, too. We hate olives. Do you like olives?"

"I do." Clint added, "Just not on my pizza."

Out of the corner of his eye, he caught Rose's warm, amused smile. Clearly, she thought he was going to fail. Which just went to show how little she really knew about him.

Clint turned his attention away from the pretty woman on the other side of the kitchen island. "Sure you kids don't want something besides cheese on yours?" he asked.

Three heads shook in unison. "Noooo way. We like cheese pizza. And nothing else. 'Cause the other stuff is way too yucky."

Clint caught the knowing look from Rose. He sent her one right back. "This is only round one," he whispered in her ear as he carried the pies, waiter-style, to the oven to be baked.

Dinner went well, but the kids were drooping with fatigue by the time they finished eating. Rose took them up to get them bathed and put to bed while he did dishes. She returned short minutes later, looking deliciously disheveled and smelling of baby shampoo and soap. "Can you believe they're already asleep?"

He took her by the hand and led her into the family room. Together they settled on the big, comfy sofa. "From the sound of it, they had a long day."

Rose tugged off her sneakers and propped her feet on the coffee table. "A lot of long days, actually."

"Any particular reason why?" he asked, watching her wriggling her toes beneath her socks.

"Part of it is the number of crops coming in now."

Figuring what the heck, he might as well get comfortable, he took off his boots and put his legs up, too. "I'm guessing winter can be a little slower?"

"Not as slow as you might think. The Texas pecan crop harvests in the fall, and we get greens and cabbage and broccoli and a lot of root vegetables year-round. Plus, last year I started selling Christmas trees and greenery for my brother-in-law."

"So you really don't get a break."

"Not much of one. Which is why I put the kids in the Montessori preschool for half days last year. This year I stepped it up to the full-day program so I can get most of my work done while they are gone." Rose raked her teeth across her soft and delicate lower lip. "The new schedule has worked well overall. The kids have a lot of friends at school, and while mornings are academically oriented, the afternoons are all fun activities and field trips."

Clint nodded. "They seem happy."

Rose got up and headed for the kitchen, returning with

a box of chocolates. "They are. The only problem is that sometimes they can get overtired and hence be really difficult to deal with. And now, as you heard earlier," she said, working off the box top and offering him dibs, "Stephen is beginning to resent living in an estrogen-powered household."

Clint selected a dark chocolate square with an almond on the top. "It can be rough being the only male sibling."

"That's right. You have four sisters and no brothers." Rose plucked up a round milk chocolate treat with a fancy curl on the top. She took a small bite, savoring the cherry nougat filling. "I forgot about that," she murmured, still sitting sideways on the sofa, facing him, her bent knee a millimeter away from nudging his thigh. "How did you survive?"

Trying not to think about what he would really like to do, which was shove the darn box of candy aside, lift her onto his lap and find pleasure in a whole *other* way, Clint tamped down his desire with effort. He admitted, "I went outside and worked on the ranch, and I rode my horse a lot."

She swallowed another small bite of her candy. "That bad, hmm?"

"At that age? Oh, yeah."

Throat dry, he watched her polish off the last of her candy. If she made love with the same dedication to pleasure she gave eating her dessert, they would have one heck of a time together. To distract himself, he took another piece of candy from the box.

"So what was the worst thing about having so many females around?" Rose asked, helping herself to another piece of candy, too.

Clint shrugged. With the last of the chocolate and caramel melting on his tongue, he forced himself to concentrate on the conversation. "It wasn't so much the fights over the bathroom or boys, or clothes, or the phone, or the car we all had to share as teenagers. It was the constant lobbying and negotiating that drove me around the bend. Or, as my mom used to say, everyone in the family wanted to give orders. No one wanted to take orders. And you can't have a tribe that's all chiefs and have peace."

Rose offered him more candy. He refused. So she set the box aside and turned to face him again. This time her bent knee did nudge his thigh.

She leaned toward him slightly. "Yet there had to be some benefit. I mean, you understand women. Whereas I don't understand men at all, mostly because I grew up without any brothers."

Shifting slightly, too, he draped his arm along the back of the couch. "So they were an alien species?"

"Something to dream over." As soon as the admission was out, she blushed.

He tugged playfully on a lock of her hair. "I kind of like the sound of that."

The color in her cheeks deepened. She sucked in a breath and scrambled to her feet. "Clint…"

Forcing himself to be the gentleman he had been raised to be, he got up, too. "I know." He stood, looking down at her, hands braced on his waist. "Time for me to go." Even if he didn't want to leave.

She escorted him to the door.

He lingered in the doorway, glad she didn't know that much about guys. 'Cause if she had, she would have known he had lovemaking on his mind.

Having given up on trying to figure out what was in her thoughts, though—at least for tonight—he did what a guy always did when he was interested in a woman. Made sure he had the next outing planned before exiting the current one.

"So what time are you and the triplets coming to the

Double Creek for dinner tomorrow night?" he asked casually.

Her delicate brow knit in surprise. "You still want to try and get them to eat their vegetables?" she asked. "Even given how your charm offensive failed?"

He watched her run back to the kitchen for the cobbler she'd intended to send home with him earlier. Their fingers brushed as she handed it over.

"I'm not sure my effort did crash and burn—entirely," he countered. After all, he'd stayed for dinner, dishes, the kids' bedtime and conversation afterward. That was definitely something.

He'd also managed to make a wager with her that would guarantee a lot more time with her over the coming days.

"Five o'clock sound okay to you?" he continued affably, determined to be as patient as it took.

She was definitely a woman worth waiting for.

Rose smiled, her pretty eyes dancing with delight. "Sounds good."

"DON'T BE SO DISCOURAGED," Rose said early Sunday evening as she watched the kids have their last hurrah post dinner on the big front porch of Clint's home. He'd brought out a Matchbox car set he'd purchased for the occasion, similar to one he'd enjoyed in his childhood, and the triplets were having a great time running the small cars over the wooden planks. "Cutting out the raw veggies in animal shapes was a great idea."

He cast a fond look at her kids. "I just wasn't the first to try it."

"It was one of my parents' old tricks."

Clint sat next to her on the chain-hung swing on one end of the porch. Intimacy simmered between them as he draped his arm along the back of it and gazed down at her. "Did it work on you?"

He looked so handsome in the fading evening light, it was all Rose could do not to snuggle into the curve of his arm. "Yes, but I never had an aversion."

"Point taken." He leaned in closer. "Well, just so you know, I'm not giving up."

He wasn't giving up on their bet—or his pursuit of her? Even though he hadn't put the moves on her, she could feel him wanting to do so. It was in every lingering look and smile.

"I can see you aren't," she said, aware they were flirting without actually flirting.

He looked deep into her eyes, promising, "And I will persevere."

Rose swallowed around the sudden parched feeling in her throat. "I hope you do," she returned huskily.

Not just because she wanted her kids eating healthier. But because she enjoyed spending time with him. And this would accomplish that.

She cleared her throat. "In the meantime, since we have a minute, did you get the email last night from the Farmtech advertising team?"

Clint nodded, some of the joy fading from his eyes.

Feeling a little guilty about pushing him into something he clearly did not want to do, Rose continued, "They invited me to be here tomorrow morning, too."

The tension left Clint's broad shoulders. "Can you be?"

She nodded. "If you want me here, sure." Anything to make the contracted work go more smoothly.

He reached over and briefly squeezed her hand. "I do."

Although she realized she was being ridiculous, she felt a little bereft when he let her fingers go. "Any particular reason why?"

Clint exhaled. The brooding look was back on his face. "Let's just say I have a gut feeling the whole experience is going to be one Texas-size pain," he said gruffly.

As IT TURNED OUT, Clint was right.

When Rose arrived, shortly after 9:00 a.m., at least forty cars clogged the lane leading to the Double Creek ranch house. Some belonged to curious co-op members and ranch equipment dealership employees who'd heard filming was about to commence and hoped—if not to end up as an extra in the commercial—at least to enjoy the excitement of watching it happen. The rest were part of the ad-agency team and photography crew.

The late May day was already hot and humid, with temperatures predicted to climb into the mid-nineties. Everyone was beginning to sweat. And already there was tension.

Clint resisted the ad director's attempt to steer him into a makeup chair. "I don't need anything on my face to sit in the air-conditioned cab of a berry picker," he said, scowling.

The set designer fumed. "You certainly need a shirt that doesn't have stains on the front of it!"

Clint looked down at his broad chest, as did Rose.

His blue-and-white plaid shirt had been washed but not ironed. Worse, faint blotches of mustard and ketchup, the remnants of the triplets' culinary disaster, could still be seen. But only if you looked up close, Rose noted. From behind the glass of the berry picker cab, it would not be noticeable.

"So I'll get another," he growled.

"Actually, maybe Clint should just take it off," the ad director suggested.

Clint looked right back at him. "You first," he drawled, deadpan.

No one on the ad team laughed.

But everyone else within earshot did.

Jeff, the owner of the dealership providing the farm equipment for the shoot, began to look alarmed.

It was time, Rose knew, for her to intervene.

"How about we all take five and regroup?" she suggested pleasantly. "I'll go in the house with Clint and help him pick out a new shirt."

"Make it several," the ad director snapped before turning to one of his assistants. "Call that Western-wear store we passed in town and see what they can get out here in his size, pronto!"

While everyone leaped into action, Rose steered Clint up the path to the ranch house, then inside. "I know this is hard," she said as they walked through the beautifully appointed home, which had been completely redone by the previous owners, then sold to him complete with furnishings.

A muscle worked in Clint's jaw. "You're not the one already being treated like a piece of meat."

"Actually, I think it's *really hot male model*," she corrected him dryly.

Nothing. He didn't even crack a smile.

"It's okay to have a little fun with this, you know."

He'd never looked sexier...or grumpier. "Not in the mood."

Okay, she thought, turning her gaze away from the tense set of his impossibly broad shoulders. Maybe she couldn't blame him for that, since none of this had been his idea. And neither of them had been at all prepared for just how much of a circus it had already turned out to be.

She turned away from him, ignoring the low, insistent quiver in her belly. Telling herself it was the fact she'd been too rushed that morning to eat much breakfast, she said calmly, "Fine. Let's see what you've got in the way of shirts."

He muttered something ungentlemanly under his breath.

She swung back to face him with a lift of her brows. It was a good thing they had dozens of people waiting on them just outside. Otherwise, no telling what would happen with the two of them closed up together. Both of them edgy and looking for an outlet for all the excess emotion...

Telling herself to forget the foolish notion of making love with Clint, Rose cleared her throat. "Unless you want the ad director up here, going through your closet and helping you?"

There was a long beat of silence.

She stared at him. He stared right back. His gaze was heated. "Save me," he blurted out.

Figuring that was as much consent as she was likely to get, Rose pivoted away from him to thumb through the selection. Along with roughly two dozen Western shirts, some old, some new, there were several business suits, plus a really nice black tuxedo with pleated white shirt, dressy black hat and boots. A lot of jeans. Another dozen or so pairs of custom boots, again in varying degrees of usage.

Looking a little James Bond–ish, he lounged against the closet frame. "Maybe I should just stroll out in a tuxedo."

Rose laughed. "Don't give them any ideas." Happy to find him in a slightly more cooperative mood, she held out a dark blue shirt for him to put on. He stripped off the old one, which gave her a nice view of his mouthwateringly good physique. Shoulders wide enough to lean on. Ripped abs and a sexy navel. Lower still, it was easy to see how well he filled out a pair of jeans.

Heat rose to her cheeks. She really had to stop this before she ended up kissing him again.

She watched as he pushed his brawny arms through the sleeves. "Why did you wear that stained shirt, anyway?" She set the offending garment aside, intending to take it home and launder out the stains her children had wrought.

His brown eyes never left hers. "Superstition. It had good karma because of what happened when I wore it last. It was my first encounter with you and your kids at your home."

Her heart skittered in her chest. "Our first kiss."

He grinned. "That, too."

Oh, my.

He shrugged and ambled closer. Threading a hand through her hair, he cupped her cheek and lifted her face to his. "It brought me good luck that day." Ever so softly, he added, "I was hoping it would do the same today."

Rose didn't know why she was so surprised. Rodeo cowboys were athletes. Athletes were superstitious, with rituals and talismans they believed brought them good luck.

Were she and the kids now part of Clint's?

And if so, how did she feel about that? As thrilled as her quickening pulse seemed to indicate?

There was no time to explore the issue, however, not with all those people waiting on them, probably wondering what the two of them were up to in here. Ignoring the inner heat the notion generated, she stepped back a pace. "You ready?"

"Just about." He finished buttoning his shirt and tucked it into the waistband of his jeans.

She looked at him again, refusing to get sucked in by the blatant sexiness of his gaze. "Try and cooperate?"

His grin widened. "No problem. As long as they don't ask me to do anything stupid."

But of course, Rose noted ruefully, the advertising team did ask him to do something foolish. Time and time and time again.

She did have to give Clint some credit for trying his best to be a good sport. He drove the berry picker up and down the rows for two solid hours without complaint as they filmed from angle after angle.

He even did his best to accommodate them when they

had him repeatedly climbing into the cab. "We need you to look happier, McCulloch!" He swung around, Stetson low across his brow, his face bearing the expression of a warrior about to head into battle. "This *is* happy," he said flatly.

Ted Trainer, the Farmtech exec on site, howled. "You're frowning!"

The ad director shook his head. For him, that was the least of the problems. "I really think the navy-blue shirt is a mistake. We need him in a cowboy plaid."

His assistant handed Clint a freshly steamed brand-new shirt from Monroe's Western Wear in town. "We need you to put this on. Now."

A half dozen other garments waited to be tried.

"And makeup! See what you can do about the sweat on his brow. Someone get the hair dryer and blow the edges of his hair dry!"

Looking like a caged lion, Clint suffered through that process over and over. He changed shirts repeatedly. Bored, the local residents drifted away.

And still the ad team worked to get just the right footage in the searing heat. Until finally even they'd had enough.

"We're going to have to come back tomorrow," Aaron, the ad director said. "We'll bring more wardrobe with us and work on the actual interview then."

Clint went still. "Interview?" He spoke as if he could not possibly have heard right.

"For the ads we're going to put on YouTube," the Farmtech exec interjected. "Figure on at least three or four hours of questions. Then we can splice from that."

Clint's scowl deepened. The uncooperative warrior was back. "On *berry picking*?"

The ad director stepped back in to say soothingly, "That, and the ease of using the machine. But not to worry. We'll throw in some questions about your rodeo days, too. How the two ventures compare."

"I don't see how they do," he said, his mouth quirking slightly.

Aaron waved off Clint's concern. "Again, don't sweat it. Our copywriting team is working on a script for you. All you have to do is memorize it or read it off cue cards."

Clint exhaled slowly and folded his arms across his chest. "And then I'll be done?"

"With the filming aspect, yeah," the director said with a nod.

The Farmtech exec added, "But you'll still have the trade shows to do."

Trade shows?

Clint slid Rose a long, level look, then turned back to the marketing director. "Excuse me?"

"You have to make appearances," Ted explained breezily. "But rest assured, we'll rehearse you. And pay you the hourly rate we agreed upon in the contract, for any time spent."

Clint turned back to Rose as soon as the group of men walked away. Accusation was blazing in his eyes, and with good reason, she thought in dismay. After all, she had been the one to instigate this whole publicity blitz!

"Did you know about this?" he demanded.

She shook her head. "Not to worry," she assured him, putting her hand on his rock-hard biceps and giving it a squeeze. "I know just who to call."

Chapter Seven

An hour later, everyone else but Rose had left, and their childhood friend and employment-law expert Travis Anderson sat on the front porch of the Double Creek ranch house, reading through the contract that Clint had signed.

Apparently as eager to have answers as Rose was, Clint looked to the lawyer for advice.

"So what do you think?" he asked in the gravelly tone she loved so much. "Can the manufacturer force me to hawk the berry picker at trade shows?"

Travis nodded. "That, and anything else related to publicity Farmtech and their ad agency dream up."

This was not what Rose had wanted to hear. She stood, hands balled at her sides, ruing the day she had ever rushed Clint into this. Had she not been so eager to save the blackberry crop and negotiate a deal, she would have realized they all needed to slow down. Take a look at the fine print. Hire lawyers and have them work it out carefully and thoroughly. But she hadn't.

And now they were in a pickle of her making.

Still hoping to find a way out, she protested, "But it doesn't say anything about that in the written agreement!"

Travis turned his narrow-eyed gaze to both of them. "Exactly the problem. The terms are so general and so vague they could be interpreted any way the farm equipment company and their legal team see fit."

Although Rose knew he had to be upset, too, Clint retained his poker face. He leaned back in his chair, shoulders pressed against the roughhewn wooden frame. "What happens if I refuse their demands?"

Frown deepening, Travis said, "You'd be in breach. They could sue you."

"Would they win?" Clint asked in an inscrutable tone.

"Given the way the terms were written, probably."

Knowing this could ruin the business deal they'd all struck, and then some, Rose clasped her hands between her jean-clad knees and leaned forward. It was still hot as heck, despite the breeze blowing across the land and the porch fan whirring above them. "You're sure?" she asked one more time, hoping some loophole had been overlooked. "There's no way out?"

Travis handed the contract back to Clint, his expression as matter-of-fact as it was grim. He stood. "Not unless the powers that be at Farmtech decide Clint wasn't what they were looking for after all."

And they all knew, as handsome and sexy as Clint was in a gruff Texas rancher way, that scenario was not likely.

His manner still as composed as hers was agitated, Clint stood. He thanked Travis, wrote him a check for his time, and walked him to his pickup truck. Rose could have left then, too.

Instead, she carried the iced-tea glasses into the ranch house kitchen, which was, she couldn't help but note, a cook's dream. The walls were a pale, masculine gray. The state-of-the-art appliances were all stainless steel, the countertops made of Carrara marble, the plentiful white cabinets outfitted with pewter pulls. An indoor grill— where Clint had cheerfully cooked hot dogs for her and the kids the day before—sat opposite the long island with half a dozen comfortable high-backed stools.

Yet it seemed empty somehow.

In need of something.

A family, maybe?

As big and bustling as the ones they had both grown up with?

Heavy male footsteps sounded behind her.

Rose turned. Clint stood framed in the doorway, and her heart leapt to her throat. Even though he was sweaty, his boots and clothes covered with a fine layer of grit from the recently plowed paths between the rows, he'd never looked better or more ruggedly sexy. To top it all off, he seemed calmer and more in control than he had all day. That prompted her to ask, "What else did Travis say?"

"What we already know." Clint massaged a hand over one shoulder, then the other. "That it's always a good idea to seek legal advice before I sign any contract."

Their eyes met and held for a breath-stealing moment. "Besides that," she prodded him.

The reserve was back in his eyes, along with the lingering desire. "Nothing."

Like heck it was nothing! Rose thought in frustration, aware she wasn't the only one erecting barriers between them now. And though he had every right to be upset with her for getting them all in this mess, she sensed it was more than that suddenly holding him back. "You can leave anytime," he drawled, crossing his arms over his broad chest as if he were having trouble corralling his emotions, too.

Which was yet another great big clue. "Not," she said, matching his newly testy tone to a T, "until you tell me what you're up to."

OF COURSE SHE would see right through him. "I don't know what you're talking about," he hedged.

She stepped closer, heat in her eyes. "You're going to try and get yourself fired. Aren't you?"

Although he was tempted to tell her everything he hadn't confided to his lawyer, Clint had no intention of doing so. He wanted Rose to have complete deniability if and when the dirt hit the fan.

"Well?" she demanded.

Shrugging noncommittally, he strode to the fridge, reached for the gallon jug of tea and poured himself another tall glass. "Shouldn't you be picking up your kids?"

"I made arrangements hours ago, when I saw how badly things were going," she informed him. "Lily and Gannon have them for the evening."

Clint wasn't surprised she'd called on her sister and his good friend. The married couple were a shining example of everything a young family should be. Their kids all got along great, too. And there would soon be another boy for Stephen to pal around with.

Unable to help himself, he rubbed at the skin beneath his shirt collar. "It's probably not too late for you to join them."

Rose stepped closer and peered intently at him. "What are those red marks on your neck?" she asked in alarm. "And the backs of your hands?"

Aware he itched so bad he was about to crawl out of his skin, Clint finished his glass of iced tea and poured another. "Obviously, I've had a reaction to the coating they put on new clothes to keep them from wrinkling."

"Oh, my heaven. I forgot about your sensitivity to that!"

He hadn't.

He'd been uncomfortable for hours now.

He reached into the cabinet and brought out the first-aid kit and a bottle of diphenhydramine. He swallowed two tablets of the antihistamine with the rest of his tea, then yanked his shirt over his head. "It'll be fine in a few hours."

Rose gasped when she saw the hives dotting his shoulders and chest. "Why didn't you say something sooner? Let the ad team know your clothes have to be laundered first!"

It had been a long time since Clint had been fussed over by a woman. He just wished it had been under other circumstances. Say, in his bedroom...

Aware she was still waiting for an answer, he returned curtly, "Because I wanted to get the filming over with." And, like an idiot, he'd been hoping this wouldn't happen.

She ran her fingers over a raised welt on his shoulder. The softness of her touch tantalized him. "You need to go to the emergency room."

He tore his eyes from the perspiration-dampened clothing sticking to her breasts. It was faint, but he could see the imprint of her nipples beneath the soft cotton cloth. "The antihistamine will take care of it."

She touched another welt, then another. Just like that, he felt himself grow hard.

Oblivious to the effect she was having on him, she asked, "What if it doesn't?"

He stepped back before he lost his mind and made love to her then and there. Doing what was best for them both, he willed the blood out of his lower extremities. "I'll deal with it, then." Throbbing with need, he stepped away.

The hurt on her face mingled with concern. "Clint—!"

The sound of his name in her low, gentle voice slammed him even more. He swung away and walked past her. Much as he might want to haul her in his arms and kiss her until she surrendered, he couldn't go there with Rose. She was not cut out for casual sex. Until the circumstances between them changed—if they *ever* changed—he had to find a way to keep her at arm's length.

Luckily for him, brusqueness and crudeness usually worked.

"Leave. Stay. I don't care." Except, damn it all, he did. "I'm going to shower now." *Before the incessant itching makes me strip naked here and now.*

Still eyeing the blotchy spots on his shoulders, arms and chest, she trailed him as far as the newel post.

"Unless you want to follow me around and watch that, too," he baited her.

She sucked in a sharp breath. Just as he had known she would.

"Or, better yet, join me…"

She stiffened, gazing at his bare chest, then his mouth. "Not. Happening. Cowboy."

He chuckled, not the least bit sorry he'd put it out there as a possibility. "Suit yourself." Crumpled shirt in hand, he gave her one last lingering glance, then climbed the stairs.

HE'D BEEN A JERK to dismiss her, and while normally Rose would have accepted the hint and gladly fled the premises, his allergic reaction had her worried.

So she remained downstairs. Pacing. Waiting. Five minutes passed. Then ten. Fifteen. And still no Clint.

How long did it take someone to shower?

It took her less than five minutes these days, if that long. But then she had three kids who could never be left unsupervised for long.

He was single. Grimy and gritty.

And very itchy.

Still, as her watch edged toward twenty minutes, she became increasingly nervous.

Especially because she could well remember the day when her sister Violet had an allergic reaction. Rose's throat grew dry. What if—just like with her sister—the situation was far more serious and deadly than anyone had realized, until it was almost too late? Panicked, Rose raced up the stairs, taking them two and three at a time. There were six bedrooms in all, and the last one, at the end of the hall—the master suite—was Clint's.

The bedroom door was wide open.

As was the door to the adjoining master bath.

A shower was running.

And maybe…some sort of radio…playing a somebody done somebody wrong country song.

"Clint?" She yelled at the doorway, rapping her knuckles hard on the wooden frame. "Clint! Are you okay in there?"

Nothing.

Rose tried again.

Still nothing. Except more running water, and more country music, and escalating fear within her.

He was probably fine.

But what if he wasn't?

Terrified now at what she might find, Rose moved across the carpet. "Clint!" she yelled again, rounding the corner.

The bathroom smelled like soap and man. Clint was standing in an elegant glass-walled shower, his body braced against the tile wall, both arms folded above him. His legs were spread. His head was down and forward slightly from the wall. Water sluiced onto his neck and shoulders from the rainfall shower fixture above, washing away the shampoo and soap before rolling down his muscular back, past his waist, to his buttocks and thighs. And, oh my, the man was built, she thought as he turned toward her in surprise and gave her a very slow and sexy smile.

Clint hadn't expected Rose would take him up on his offer. But now that she was here, he was all in, too.

He opened the stall door. Giving her no chance to

change her mind, he tugged her inside with him, threaded his hands through her hair and lowered his mouth to hers.

He expected her to kiss him back tentatively and wonderingly, not surge against him wildly.

He expected her to have second thoughts once again. Not slide her hands around his back and press him intimately against her. Kiss him fiercely, evocatively, until they were both groaning for more.

A rush of need coursed through him, and the anger and frustration he'd felt all day at last began to ease. This was what he needed, he realized as her hips rocked restlessly against him. *She* was what he needed. And damn it all, he thought as her soft, pliant body surrendered all the more, if she didn't realize it, too.

Rose hadn't expected any of this, but she couldn't fight it, either, not when the feel of him pressed against her sent her spinning. She hadn't been close to anyone in so long, she thought, savoring the moment with everything she possessed. Hadn't ever felt this much a woman. Or wanted a man with such ardor. But she wanted Clint—in her arms, in her bed, in her life. She wanted him to fill her up and end the aching loneliness deep inside her. To help her live again, really live. And if this was the way it happened, feeling him grow rock-hard against her even as the water cascaded down on top of them, so be it.

He was hot. The water was cold—deliberately, she guessed. Her body was on fire. "Your rash…" she whispered.

He touched her erect nipples. "…is fading. The cold water helps."

Not everything, she noted breathlessly. Not the pounding of her heart.

Or the raging, tingling need.

Or the sense that it would be ever so easy to fall recklessly in love with him.

Especially when he was dropping his head and kissing

her again, hot and hard and wet and deep. Then slowly, sweetly and tenderly, until she moved impatiently against him, wanting still more. With a husky laugh, he slipped off her T-shirt and her bra, removed her boots and unsnapped her jeans. She quivered as denim and panties slid down her thighs. Her hands rested on his broad shoulders while he helped her step out.

"So beautiful," he murmured, his thumbs tracing the curves of her breasts before gently caressing her tender nipples. "So smokin' hot."

As was he.

She had never imagined such male perfection. Or wicked sensuality. Never imagined feeling so wanton herself...

Still kneeling, he savored the sight of her and pressed a kiss to her most sensitive spot. Hands cupping his head, she arched against him, yearning to feel everything with him. He parted her thighs, found her with his fingertips, and kissed her again until she clung to him like a lifeline. She was aware even as he found her that she was on the brink. And then his mouth was on her again, and she was gone, floating, free. Knowing it had happened way too soon.

"Clint," she rasped, sorry now she'd sped on ahead, aware she had never felt pleasure that intense.

But he didn't look unhappy as he rose above her. Instead, he was smiling like he'd won the championship.

His head lowered, her hands clutched his biceps, and she shuddered at the tender intimacy of their connection. "We're just getting started," he said.

He kissed her breast, making good on that promise, letting his tongue slide over the nipple.

Then he exited the shower just long enough to retrieve a condom. She watched, mesmerized, as he rolled it on. Then he settled her against the wall. Her legs wrapped around his hips. A shaky breath escaped her. And then they were kissing again, as if the kiss was an end in itself. He kissed her possessively, with exquisite gentleness and precision.

She was wet and open. He was hot and hard. And then there was no more waiting, no more wondering what it would feel like to have him inside her. For the first time in her life, she lost herself completely in passion and desire. He was just as intent on giving her what she needed, the size of him filling and stretching, thrusting into her over and over.

She loved being with him like this, feeling like he was hers, just for this moment. Loved hoping he would not eventually realize her life was so chaotic that she would never have enough time for him…and abandon her, just like her ex had. But even as they took each other to the very height of bliss, she knew that very well could happen.

Her body still quivering with aftershocks, Rose slumped against Clint, knowing she had never felt this physically content and well-loved. Nor been as worried about what was potentially a huge mistake.

A sigh of wistfulness swept through her.

Clint smoothed a hand over her wet hair. He pressed a kiss to her temple, his body still as damp and shuddery as hers. "What are you thinking?" he murmured in her ear.

Rose drew a deep breath, still trying to calm her racing heart. She extricated their bodies, moved past him and stepped out of the stall, gathering up her clothes as she went. Aware he was still waiting, she forced herself to look into his eyes and say what was on her mind. "The truth? That this wasn't what I intended when I came up here."

Chapter Eight

Talk about a kick in the gut. Especially after the no-holds-barred way they had just made love. Clint shut off the water, grabbed a towel and wrapped it around his waist. "What do you mean, it wasn't what you intended?"

She shimmied into her wet panties and slipped her bra on. He stepped behind her to fasten the clasp, his fingers brushing her silky soft skin.

Her back still to him, she snatched up her shirt and slipped her arms through the sleeves. "The only reason I barged in here was because I thought you might have passed out or gone into anaphylactic shock or something."

Well, that was a new one.

Spinning around, she caught the look of wry amusement on his face.

He didn't know why she wouldn't just admit she'd come up there to join him in the shower and, now that it was over, had second thoughts about it. Just the way she had when they'd kissed.

"It's not that far out in left field," she said as she tugged on her jeans. Which wasn't easy, given how wet they were. He grew hard again, watching her wiggle and pull.

Deciding it might be a good idea for him to get dressed, too, he walked into the bedroom. Grabbed a pair of boxer briefs, then a clean pair of jeans. "I told you all I had was a simple contact allergy rash."

"I know that." She sauntered into the bedroom, cowgirl boots and soggy socks in hand. "But sometimes things happen."

Yeah. Sometimes things happened. People made love. And didn't run from the consequences after.

Oblivious to the lusty nature of his thoughts, she let her glance fall to the pants he was pulling on. The arousal he'd been trying to ease sprang back to life.

She turned away, the color in her cheeks letting him know she had noticed. Swallowing, she set her boots down on the floor and slid her bare feet into them. Beneath her wet blouse and bra, her nipples pearled.

"Such as…?" he drawled. It was all he could do not to reach out, haul her right back into his arms and show her all over again what incredible chemistry the two of them had.

"Things like medical emergencies," Rose said heatedly.

Clint blinked and, for both their sakes, tried to harden his heart. "You thought I was having one?"

She lifted her chin and locked eyes with him. "I worried it could be a possibility."

She was serious. He came closer, listening.

"As it turns out, my sister Violet is extremely allergic to bee stings, but no one knew it until the first time she got stung. If my parents hadn't both been doctors and had EpiPen injectors in their medical bags, she probably would have died before we ever got her to the hospital."

The chalky color on Rose's face let him know how traumatic that had been for her, and still was to this day.

He zipped up his jeans. Then, barefoot, bare-chested, he moved toward her. Determined to comfort her yet again, he murmured, "I'm sorry." He cupped her shoulders so she wouldn't bolt and looked down at her. "I didn't know that."

Her gaze fell to his chest. For a moment she looked as if she were tempted to run her fingers through the mat of hair spreading across his pecs and down to his fly—the way she had when they'd made love—but then she swallowed and took another deep, quavering breath. "Anyway, you were up here so long, and that rash had looked so awful when you left, that my imagination ran wild."

So had his, but not for the reason she thought. Which was yet another motivation for him staying so long in the icy shower. He'd needed to cool off. Tamp down the desire to make her his. And look how well *that* had turned out...

He wanted her to be his woman more than ever.

But did she feel the same way about him? The tension coiling inside him once again, he tucked a hand beneath her chin and lifted her face to his. "Well, now you know." He rubbed his thumb across the curve of her lower lip. "I always take long showers." It was one of the luxuries in this life he regularly afforded himself. Although they were usually hot and steamy, not ice-cold.

Rose nodded. Something mysterious came and went in her green eyes. Finally she said, "I have to go home and change clothes and then go over to Lily's and get my kids. But before I go—" she swallowed "—I need to ask. Can we please just chalk this up to yet another of my grand mistakes and forget this ever happened?"

GRAND MISTAKES? JUST when he thought it couldn't get any worse, it did. Wanting to understand her, Clint grabbed a clean shirt from his closet. "What were the others?"

He accompanied her into the hall.

Soft lips twisted into a frown, she started down the staircase, grabbing her purse and key ring on the way out. "The biggest was marrying a man I should only have had an affair with. Because in truth, all Barry and I ever really had was passion, and at the end, we didn't even have that." Slinging her bag onto her shoulder, she stepped onto the front porch.

He watched her sort through the keys until she found the ignition key for her Rose Hill Farm pickup truck. He said, "Yet you had three kids together."

Her chin lifted in the stubborn way he was beginning to know so well. "Because I wanted a baby. Barry never did." Sighing, she looked off into the distance, toward the setting sun. "But he said he would be okay with it if I took the majority of the responsibility and did all the parenting."

"And you were satisfied with that?"

She swung back to face him. "No, but I thought he'd feel different once our baby was born." She released a breath and looked down at her hands. "Then it turned out to be triplets." Another sigh, deeper this time. "And all Barry ever felt was trapped and overwhelmed," she recounted sadly. "Or, as he told me on the day he left us, raising kids just wasn't his thing. And he'd prefer not to be involved."

"What a jerk. You and the triplets deserved better." Clint leaned against one of the posts holding up his porch roof. She looked so disappointed that his heart ached for her. "Where is he now?"

"The northeast somewhere, climbing the corporate ladder, but I really don't know much more than that. The child-support checks he sends me are delivered via the state of Texas." Exhaling wearily, Rose pushed the damp curls off her face. "Right now it's not an issue for the kids. They haven't yet started clamoring for a daddy, but eventually that will happen, and I'll have to help them understand that's not a realistic wish under the circumstances."

It could be, Clint thought.

He, for one, would love to be daddy to her kids.

If their momma loved him.

And right now, given the wall she had around her heart, it wasn't likely Rose would let him—or any guy—in.

On the other hand, he had faced tougher challenges in his life. And now that he'd experienced the magic of making love with her, he was even more motivated to break down those barriers.

He studied her closely. "And you blame yourself for this situation you're all in?" Despite the fact she could hardly be comfortable in her soggy clothing, she perched on the porch railing, one foot flat on the wooden floor, the other bent toward her calf.

"I hold myself accountable for not being realistic from the get-go, yes." She continued, recollecting unhappily, "You see, I found out the hard way that, for a union to be a success, you have to be on the same page as your spouse on pretty much everything before you ever walk down the aisle together. Otherwise, you're just speeding toward disaster."

"You don't think opposites can attract?"

She gave him a look that said they had just more than proved that. "Sure—until they flame out."

She stood again and spread her hands wide. "The point is, Clint, five years ago I was starry-eyed as could be. I thought if I met Barry halfway and only got pregnant once, he'd meet *me* halfway and love the baby—or, as it turned out, all three of our children—as much as I did." Suddenly, her voice caught. "Unfortunately, Barry couldn't change any more than I could. So we never got our happily-ever-after, and the disappointment of it all was enough to make me forever cautious."

"Which is why your attempt to date again didn't work out," he surmised, sensing how devastated she had felt during her marriage and subsequent divorce. *The impact her ex's desertion must have had on her.* "Because you weren't really sure you wanted to put yourself back out there, and be that vulnerable again, in the first place."

She shook her head in a way that let him know he wasn't

quite right. "It takes time and energy and commitment to build a relationship that will endure. Realistically, I don't have that, and won't until my kids are grown." Clamping her arms in front of her as if warding off a sudden chill, she blurted, "And I don't want to be pressured or made to feel guilty for what I can or cannot give."

Clint could understand that. He moved closer, his heart filling with a depth of feeling he didn't expect.

"And now the situation is reversed," she said, a mixture of sorrow and discouragement lacing her low tone. "You're the one looking to get married and settle down and have kids." She paused to look him in the eye with the kindness and compassion he had come to expect from her.

She took his hand, squeezed it briefly. "And you deserve to have that—and the big, all-encompassing love that goes hand in hand with every successful marriage, and serves as the solid foundation for every happy family."

Clint's lips twisted ruefully. Well, at least she got that much about him, he thought.

She released his hand and pivoted toward the steps.

He followed her to her pickup truck. Watched as she unlocked it and tossed her handbag inside. "What about you? Shouldn't you have all that, too?" he asked huskily.

Rose climbed into the driver's seat. One arm resting on the steering wheel, she turned to face him. "Minus the spouse, I'm already there. At least as much as my previous mistakes will allow." She reached for her shoulder harness, dragged it across the soft swell of her breasts and clasped the buckle. "I have my kids. My business, my home. And most of all, my independence. Because…" She turned the key in the ignition, and the motor started with a purr. "If there was one thing my brief foray into dating showed me, it's that I don't want to get married again."

He studied the just-made-love glow about her, knowing

he emanated the same. Which made her swift change in mood all the more baffling. "Meaning what?" he asked.

"Meaning that as nice as making love with you was," she said, looking deep into his eyes, "for both our sakes—yours especially—this can never happen again."

IT HARDLY SEEMED POSSIBLE, Rose noted with increasing frustration, but the second day of filming went worse than the first. Clint wore only pre-laundered garments this time, thanks to her timely intervention with the wardrobe person the evening before. But the day was overcast, and they were never able to get the light just right. Or make the berry picker look like a must-have piece of farm machinery as they wanted.

Most troubling of all was the crankiness of the star.

The usually affable Clint was grim and impatient more often than not. He had almost nothing to say to Rose. And on the rare occasions the director was able to get him to crack a smile, he looked like someone who'd been forced to pose for endless family photos when he had somewhere else he wanted to be.

Rose knew she was at least partially responsible for Clint's bad mood, because of how things had ended between them last night. Truth to tell, she was feeling a little cranky and out of sorts, maybe even a little dejected, too.

She kept wondering if she'd made a mistake, calling it quits so hastily. Yet the pragmatic side of her, the side that didn't want either of them to get hurt, knew she had done the prudent thing in protecting them both.

Not that Clint felt any gratitude to her, for that...

Worse, the actual berry picking was at a minimum. After two days of this, the vines were exploding with fruit that would soon go bad if they didn't get it picked. Deciding something had to be done about that, Rose headed for the execs conversing next to the stretch limousine that had carried them all out to the ranch.

Instead of being irked by the interruption, they looked glad to see her.

Glances were exchanged all around.

Then Jeff strode toward her. "Rose!" He clapped a hand on her shoulder and brought her into the huddle. "Just the person we wanted to see!"

CLINT DIDN'T KNOW what was going on in the circle of conferencing executives, but whatever it was, Rose was now at the heart of it. Just as she had been from the beginning of this circus.

Vexed to find himself in the same situation that had ended his relationship with Reba, Clint headed for his pickup truck. Thank God he had other work to do—work he *wanted* to do—or he'd lose his mind.

He'd just reached the door when Rose caught up with him, looking determined and feisty as ever. "Got a minute?"

Clint struggled to control his temper. "I've got horses and cattle to see to." All of which were currently parked at Gannon's ranch, with the Bar M horses and cattle he was also caring for.

"I understand."

Did she? Clint had to wonder. Because if she had any clue how much he hated the disruption to his normal routine, she never would have asked him to do all this.

"I just wanted to let you know the film crew won't be back again until next Monday," she continued.

Clint grimaced at her unchecked enthusiasm. "How is that good news?"

"It means you have a five-day reprieve."

Past pretending he was okay with any of this, he shrugged. "Or a sword hanging over my head."

She paused, looked away a long moment, then finally turned back to him, her remarkably cagey expression still giving him absolutely no clue what was really going on. "Would you like to come to my house for dinner this evening?"

Was this invitation connected to the recent confab beside the limousine? Or was it more personal, due to the fact she felt as aggravated as he did about them making hot, sexy, mind-blowing love and then going their separate ways?

Her sweet smile provided no answer. Sighing, he took off his hat and shoved a hand through his hair. After a day spent in the hot spring sun, he really needed a shower. And a shave. "I couldn't get there until seven-thirty."

"Perfect. You can see the triplets for half an hour before bedtime. You and I can eat and talk after that."

Hmm. An adult dinner—for two—with children sleeping upstairs. Clint felt better and more relaxed already. "Want me to bring anything?" he asked.

She flashed another smile, even warmer this time. "Just yourself."

Clint hurried through his chores. Went back to the ranch, showered, shaved and decided to slap on some aftershave lotion, too. It was nearly dark when he arrived at Rose Hill Farm. The triplets were racing around in their pajamas.

"We feel sorry for you," Scarlet announced after hello hugs and high-five's were exchanged.

Stephen nodded. "Mommy's making you lots of vegtables."

"Yeah," Sophia whispered shyly, "you're going to have to eat 'em, Mr. Clint. 'Cause you're company. And when you're company, you got to be polite."

Rose wafted by in a drift of perfume. A mischievous

look on her lovely face, she murmured, "Too bad you didn't win your wager. Or you could have shared…"

Clint chuckled, using the opportunity to give her a brief hug hello, too. Eyes holding her gaze, he warned her softly, "Oh, I haven't given up." Not on their bet.

And not on you.

A hint of color spread across her cheeks. "Then you have your work cut out for you."

Still speaking in a code the kids would not understand, he accepted a couple of carrot sticks from the canapé plate Rose held out for him. "When I set my mind to something, I can usually win." Then he made a show of really enjoying his crudités.

Happy he was playing along with her messaging, Rose grinned in approval. "I've heard that about you. It's why you were so great in rodeo, isn't it? Because you weren't afraid to build all those strong muscles by eating healthily?"

Unfortunately, the triplets were on to another subject already. They settled on the sofa next to him while he continued enjoying his raw veggies. "Mr. Clint, which game is better?" Sophia asked. "Baby dolls or engineer?"

Rose brought him a glass of iced tea to go with his appetizer. "Their cousin Henry's grandparents have an old-fashioned steam train as part of their wedding ranch business. When the triplets visit, they get to ride in the train and pretend they are driving it."

"Sounds cool!" Clint said. He wouldn't mind doing that himself, especially if he, Rose and the kids all went together.

"See!" Stephen crowed, triumphant.

Clint wordlessly offered all three kids a celery stick. All three refused. He added, "But playing baby dolls is good, too."

Scarlet sat cross-legged on the coffee table directly in

front of him. "Did you play baby dolls when you were little, Mr. Clint?"

"Unfortunately," he replied with a disgruntled sigh before he could censor himself. Catching Rose's chiding look, he went on, "I have four sisters, and they liked to play house and wedding a lot. So I was always getting drafted as either the daddy or the husband."

Rose rolled her eyes and quipped, "Which probably explains why it's taken you so long to marry as an adult. That whole endlessly reenacted wedding thing…"

"Hey," Clint protested, aware he hadn't felt this relaxed and happy in a long time, "I'll be a groom soon." Just as soon as he got the right woman to say "I do."

As expected, Rose was giving no opinion on the subject, and she swung away before he could see the expression on her face. The kids were not so circumspect. They looked at him, then their mom, then back at him. Finally Scarlet tackled the elephant in the room and spoke up. "Mr. Clint? Are you going to marry our mommy?"

ROSE BLUSHED. GIVEN the task she had ahead of her, she should have waited until the kids were sound asleep to invite Clint over. He probably wouldn't have minded having dinner with her—or even dessert and coffee—at eight-thirty.

But she hadn't done it that way. Mainly because she had wanted to remind him what her life was really like on a daily basis. However, she hadn't figured they would bring up the subject of marriage in conjunction with him.

Clint sent her an ornery grin. "Careful, kids. I don't think your mommy likes the *M* word."

Three little heads tilted in unison. Confusion reigned.

Relieved they had no idea what was really going on, she explained, "Mr. Clint is teasing."

"Oh." Her children recovered quickly. They turned back to Clint. "Will you play a game with us?"

Rose nixed the suggestion with a shake of her head. "It's bedtime."

"Maybe next time," he promised.

"Maybe means no." Sophia pouted.

Quickly Clint conceded, "Okay. You're right. We'll all *definitely* play a game together next time." This would give him another excuse to come over and spend time with all of them. And, of course, step up his plan to pursue Rose.

"Baby dolls or engineer?" Stephen persisted.

Clint threw out the first unisex thing that came to mind. "Superheroes."

Thankfully, that satisfied them.

Rose gathered up the children. All three said goodnight to Clint, then went upstairs with their mom. A short time later she returned, beckoning him into the kitchen. She, too, had showered since arriving home. Her chin-length hair had been dried into a sleek bob with a fringe of bangs across her forehead. She wore little makeup, but she didn't really need it, given how gorgeous she looked. Grabbing her floral apron off the hook on the wall, she slipped it over her head and tied it around the waist. Peering up at him impishly, she went over to the oven and lifted out a tray of sumptuous-looking barbecued chicken.

"Exactly how do you play Superheroes?"

He bypassed the island and captured her in his arms. "Haven't a clue. Luckily I have time to figure it out." Then he lowered his head and kissed her tenderly.

Rose caught her breath even as she softened against him. She splayed her hands over his chest. "What was that for?"

He gave her waist another playful squeeze before letting her go. "Practicing." He returned her look of surprise with exaggerated seriousness. "In case I'm enlisted as the groom in the next game of Wedding."

She laughed despite herself. "Very funny."

Clint walked back around the island so he wouldn't be tempted to kiss her some more. "You never know." He sat down to watch her cook. "So why did you ask me over tonight?"

He couldn't help but think, by the slightly jumpy way she was acting now, that she had some ulterior motive other than friendship.

The way she averted her gaze confirmed it. "I felt— feel—bad about the way things ended between us last night," she said finally.

"Me, too." He'd wanted her to stay. Make love with him again. Or at least not regret it…and declare it out-of-bounds for the future. "What else?"

Rose slid a green salad out of the fridge. "I get tired of eating kid food all the time, and I don't like to go to all the trouble to cook adult food just for myself."

He could buy that. He couldn't see the kids eating salad with field greens, fresh orange slices, green onions and almonds. Nor did he imagine they were crazy about the zucchini, corn and red-pepper side dish she had prepared to go along with the mashed red potatoes coming out of the oven. "And I was asked to talk to you." She brought out two place settings and put them on the island.

"By…?"

Rose brought all the dishes over and set them within reach. "Jeff Johnston and all the executives involved in the ad campaign." She whisked off her apron and settled on the stool next to him. "They're concerned about the way things are going so far." She inclined her head, indicating he should serve himself first.

Clint added the delicious-looking chicken and veggies to his plate, then watched while she did the same. "If Farmtech wanted an actor as spokesperson, they should have hired one."

She spread a napkin across her lap with extraordinary care. "They didn't want a generic pretend-farmer, Clint. They wanted you."

He tried not to admire the narrow stretch of silky-smooth thigh between her knee and the hem of her shorts. "What about you, Rose?" He lifted his gaze, taking in a brief but pleasurable glimpse of her slender waist and full breasts before returning to her face. "What do you want?"

"For this to go smoothly," she said, as if he needed reminding. "And it's *not*."

"And you're disappointed."

She stared at him, two high spots of color on her cheeks. "It occurred to me you could be trying to get fired in order to get out of whatever other contractual demands Farmtech makes."

That was, as a matter of fact, exactly what he had been attempting to do. However, still wanting her shielded from any trouble he made for himself, he took a bite of tender, succulent chicken. "Why is that your problem?"

Rose forked up a slice of orange. Then put it down again. Huffing out a breath, she looked him in the eye. "Because if you get fired, Clint, Jeff and Farmtech will take the berry picker back immediately, and all those berries will go to waste."

A fact that would break her heart.

Not sure he liked coming second to any business venture, no matter what it was, Clint met her level gaze. "And your business loses the revenue you stand to get if you harvest the crop."

She resumed eating. "As do you."

Suddenly as ticked off as she was, he sat back. "So either I straighten up and fly right, or you and I are…what?" he demanded gruffly, not sure whether he wanted to haul her into his lap and kiss her. Or simply accept that their priorities were too different, get up and leave. "No longer friends?"

Chapter Nine

Rose looked at him and sighed. "Of course we would still be friends," she declared, her emotions suddenly as fired up as his. "Unless you don't want to be?"

Clint wanted to be a whole lot more than friends, but pushing her now on that front, would get him nowhere. "What are you asking me to do?" he asked.

"Cooperate wholeheartedly," she said. "Barring that, get a third party to run interference for you so there's a buffer between you and the creative team."

This had a really familiar ring to it. He took another bite of chicken. The sauce-covered meat melted in his mouth. "Do you have anyone in mind?"

Rose went back to eating, too. "I suppose you could ask Travis, since he is your attorney, but then you'd be paying his hourly rate, and that would be expensive. Or perhaps you could get an agent..."

"An agent would take 15 percent—of everything."

Rose stiffened in surprise. "Okay. Well, I didn't know that."

Her upright posture emphasized the soft swell of her breasts. His body hardened in response.

Oblivious to what he was thinking—and *feeling*—she mused, "Then maybe an attorney would be the less expensive way to go, since this isn't anything you intend to do long-term."

Casually he baited her, "Unless more offers come up."

Rose lifted a forkful of mashed potatoes. "I suppose that could happen," she said absent-mindedly.

Clint chewed thoughtfully for a few moments, then swallowed. "But there would be more of a chance of that if I had someone advocating on my behalf," he said softly, looking her in the eye.

She nodded, distracted, then tilted her head at him. "It wouldn't have to be an agent per se, would it?"

And here it comes, he thought. *The pitch I never wanted to hear, especially from her.* He lifted his shoulders in a casual shrug. "Just someone who knows me and knows the business." He paused to let his words sink in. "Someone who would have only my best interests at heart."

Rose nodded in all innocence, suddenly looking so happy and content she was almost glowing. "Right."

Anger churned in his gut. If only she weren't the most beautiful woman he'd ever seen. "Like you?"

ROSE DIDN'T NEED to hear the soft accusation in his voice to realize he'd misunderstood her. She stopped with her fork halfway to her mouth. "What are you talking about?"

"Would you do this for me if I asked you?"

Well, that was a loaded question if she'd ever heard one! He seemed to want to know whose side she was on. His, naturally! "Yes."

"Exactly what I thought." Clint stood abruptly. "Thanks for dinner."

She blocked his way to the door. "Wait! Clint! What's going on? Why are you so angry?"

"Because I've been down this road before, Rose, and I have no intention of ever going there again." He stepped past her.

She grabbed his elbow. When he wouldn't turn toward her, she moved around him and let out a quavering breath.

"Okay, now you really have to tell me what is going on, because this is just not fair."

He narrowed his eyes at her and then continued onto the front porch. "My ex wanted to build my career, too."

Rose stepped out beside him. "She was an agent?"

"She wanted to be," he admitted with a grudging nod. "But to do that, she needed to find someone to represent first. And with my looks and my rodeo stardom, she figured the sky was the limit."

Rose picked up on the sarcasm. "I gather she was successful?"

Giving another terse shake of his head, Clint stuffed his hands in the pockets of his jeans. "She got me the saddle soap and the leather glove ads. Which, combined with the winnings I had racked up, enabled me to buy back the Double Creek."

"So what happened after that?"

Clint exhaled and cast a look at the expansive black velvet sky overhead. It was studded with stars and a brilliant three-quarter moon. "I told her I was in love with her and wanted to marry her and move back here and raise a family."

"She said no?"

Bitterness turned down the corners of his lips. "She'd fallen in love with a rodeo star. If I wanted to go with the announcing gig she had managed to drum up for me and work on developing a broadcasting career, fine. Otherwise," he shook his head grimly, "she wasn't interested."

Rose paced the porch. "And that's why you broke up."

Clint leaned against a post, a mixture of regret and lingering disappointment on his handsome face. "I don't mind being in business with a spouse. I think that can be a good thing. But Reba's idea of a rich life, and mine, were completely opposite."

Whereas, Rose thought, she suspected her and Clint's

ideas of what really counted were the same. Friends, family. Work they enjoyed. Maybe even great sex, if and when the opportunity arose…

She swallowed hard. "I'm sorry you went through that, Clint. Really I am. But that's not what I was trying to do here. The only reason I got involved at all was…"

"What?" he prodded her.

"Jeff Johnston and the Farmtech execs thought I might be able to sweet-talk you into having a better attitude."

A flash of anger glimmered in his eyes.

Rose could hardly blame him. Although her intentions were good—she'd simply been trying to bring peace to the situation—on the surface it did sound manipulative. She edged closer, breathing in the fresh-air scent of his skin. "I tried to tell them you're not the kind of guy who listens to anyone unless he wants to."

Clint waited.

Wishing she could comfort him physically without it meaning or leading to anything, she said, "But they seemed to think that…"

He shifted his gaze to her lips. "There's something going on between us?"

She felt herself flushing. "Something like that. Of course, I told them that wasn't the case, either—"

He moved brusquely away from her. "So you fibbed."

She had no choice but to follow him down the steps. "Given all that was at stake, I promised that I would talk to you."

With a sardonic lift of his brow, he pivoted toward her. "And make me a very nice dinner."

"No," she corrected hastily. "The dinner was my idea! I knew what a hard day you'd had, and I was just trying to be nice."

"Nice," he repeated.

"I was trying to be your friend. And I'd still like to be that if you'd let me."

Clint gave her a long look that she couldn't begin to interpret. "Got any dessert?" he asked finally.

The question was so far from what she'd expected, she couldn't help but laugh. "As a matter of fact, I do. So, what do you say, now that all our cards are on the table?" She held out her hand.

He took it.

"Can we start the evening over?"

Wrapping his arm around her shoulders, he reeled her in close and murmured, "I don't see why not."

VIOLET EXCHANGED HUMOROUS glances with Lily and Poppy, then elbowed Rose the next day, as the four of them toured the estate of their late grandparents, John and Lilah McCabe. "I thought I was the one who always had circles under my eyes from lack of sleep," she teased.

Rose made a face at her triplet. "Just because I'm not a resident physician does not mean I can't stay up all night, too."

Always in mommy mode these days—when she wasn't actively working as an attorney mediator— Lily put her hand on her swollen tummy. "Is one of your kids sick?" she asked Rose worriedly.

"No. Everyone's fine."

Poppy—who was working on the interior-design plans for the newly sanctioned home of the nonprofit McCabe House—set her clipboard down. She sat down midrise of the sweeping ranch house staircase. "Then why were you up all night?"

Lily and Violet sat down on the risers, as well. "We'd like to hear the answer to that, too," Violet said.

Rose sighed. If she couldn't confide in her sisters, who could she talk to? "It was Clint."

A contemplative silence fell. "He slept over?" Poppy asked.

"No. Of course not. The kids were there."

"Right." Lily nodded, knowing firsthand what it was like to juggle the whole kids and romance thing.

Not that Rose and Clint were having a romance, she reminded herself firmly. *Yet*, anyway.

Poppy grinned as if reading Rose's mind. The oldest and most forward-thinking of all the McCabe daughters, she saw no reason ever to get married. "You want him to sleep over?"

You have no idea.

Lacing her hands around her knee, Rose sidestepped the query. "We're not even dating."

"From what Gannon says, you could be," Lily put in.

Since Clint and Gannon were best buddies, Lily probably knew the scoop. "What do you mean?" Rose asked. Had Clint said something to Gannon?

"Gannon thinks Clint is really interested in you." Lily waved a hand. "Of course there's the whole you're-never-getting-married-again thing, when all Clint wants is to find The One and tie the knot."

Violet gave Lily an attagirl pat on the back. "Nicely summarized, sis."

Poppy asked, "So why was Clint keeping you up 'til all hours?"

Why indeed? Rose thought back to the long, increasingly intimate conversation that had continued through dessert, and dishes, and then cups of hot tea… "We were talking."

"Oh. *Talking*." Poppy smirked. "C'mon, Rose. Were you really just shooting the breeze, or were you making out, too?"

Everyone laughed. Rose tried, and failed, to contain

the heat moving from the center of her chest to her face. "I'm going to plead the Fifth on that one," she said dryly.

Although the truth was, they hadn't kissed.

She *had* wanted to kiss, because she positively ached to feel his lips on hers again, but Clint was the perfect gentleman all night long. Apparently he'd been respecting her boundaries. Boundaries she now yearned to break down.

Her sisters studied the shifting expressions on her face. Everyone laughed again.

Lily stood. "Well, I for one hope you do open your heart and get married again. Take it from me, sis. There's nothing like making a commitment and sharing your life with the man of your dreams."

Rose knew that.

She also realized she had made a terrible mistake once, and that one day Barry's desertion would come to hurt her children. Therefore, she didn't want them to count on Clint as anything other than yet another family friend. She might lose him, too, if things did not work out the way her starry-eyed sisters hoped.

So it was probably best they kept things casual.

"When are you going to see him again?" Violet asked, cutting into her thoughts.

Not sure how she'd let him talk her into it, Rose sighed. "Tonight. We have a bet he's just itching to win."

"Hi, Mr. Clint. How come you're wearing a costume?" Stephen asked hours later when Rose opened the door.

Actually, Rose thought, admiring the handsome, dashing way Clint looked, it was only part of one. He wore his usual jeans and boots, but instead of a button-up, he had on a gray knit T-shirt with a big red-and-yellow *S* printed on the front. A large red cape was tied around his neck. And as a finishing touch, he had a large shopping bag in one hand and a small cooler marked Superhero First-Aid Kit in the other.

Clint winked at the kids, explaining, "I'm here to play the Superheroes game with you-all."

Cheers of excitement went up from the younger crowd.

"Do we get costumes, too?" Scarlet asked.

"You sure do." Clint brought out a stack of similar T-shirts and began passing them out. Superboy went to Stephen. Supergirl shirts went to Sophia and Scarlet. "And for you, Mommy," Clint said, handing over the last, "Superwoman!"

Aware he was going to be very hard to resist if he kept up a charm offensive like this, Rose demurred. "I didn't know I was going to be playing."

He caught her hand and pulled her to his side. "It won't be nearly as much fun unless you do."

And fun was the goal for the evening.

"Then I'm in," Rose said.

The kids were already tugging the shirts on over their heads.

Clint looked at Rose, desire in his eyes, mischief curving the corners of his lips. "Need a hand with yours?"

Ha, ha. Her insides fluttered at the memory of the first time he'd helped her out of her clothing. The lovemaking that had followed might have been ill-advised, but it was still spectacular. "I think I can do it," she said drolly. Her pulse pounding with excitement, she tugged the shirt on over the yellow short-sleeved tee she was already wearing. "Now what?"

Clint opened the shopping bag again. With a flourish he brought out four capes—three tyke-size, another that was just her size.

"Well, first we put on our capes." He hunkered down and helped everyone fasten the red garments around their necks.

"And then we go outside together to hunt down the villains. Okay, Superfamily," Clint said. "Let's go!"

Together the five of them swooped outside. Clint spread the edges of his cape wide on either side of him. "Come on, everyone, time to fly!" He zoomed on ahead, swaying back and forth, pretending he was soaring like a bird in the air. Everyone followed suit.

"I don't see any villains!" Stephen shouted, really getting into the game.

Clint adapted his pace so all could catch up. "Keep looking!" he shouted over his shoulder.

Around and around the bungalow they went until Clint came to an abrupt stop.

Peeking out of one of the gardenia bushes was a garden scarecrow like the ones sold in Susie Carrigan's landscaping center. The four-foot doll with rag-mop hair and a denim and plaid ensemble appeared to be looking out at them. Without warning, Clint clutched his chest dramatically and fell down. He sprawled on the grass in front of the gardenia bush.

"What's wrong, Mr. Clint?" Sophia was the first to reach him.

Weakly, Clint pointed in the direction of the gardenia. Inside a clear plastic jar was what looked to be green jelly beans. "It's…kryptonite…!" he gasped. "It's making… me…so…weak…"

"What should we do?" Stephen asked quickly.

Clint clutched his chest. "I need…the antidote! It's in the superhero first-aid cooler!"

"I'll get it!" Beginning to see where this might be going, Rose raced back inside. She returned and set it down on the grass beside the still writhing and moaning Clint.

"Open it," he rasped.

Rose did as directed. She and the kids looked inside.

Clint gasped. "I need...the green beans! Quick! Give me three of them...before I—!"

Rose opened the container. "Better do as he says," she told the triplets soberly.

"Help me sit up," Clint grunted when they had three in hand.

Rose knelt behind him and pretended to push his broad shoulders upright. Which was easier imagined than done, given how big and solidly muscled he was. Still hamming it up, Clint held out his hand. The kids solemnly put the veggies in his palm.

"Here...goes..." He ate one. Then another. Then a third. Slowly he began to look and act normal.

Finally he said, "I think I'm all better. Yep, the veggies worked to fight off the kryptonite." A big smile spread across his face. "I'm only glad that no one else..." He turned to look at Rose. Getting the gist of what he wanted her to do, she too collapsed dramatically on the grass beside Clint. "Is it the kryptonite?" he gasped, leaning over her.

Feebly, Rose nodded.

"Kids!" Clint shouted. "You know what to do!"

And so it went. Rose ate her green beans—and survived. Then Scarlet fell ill. She too had to eat three green beans. As did the similarly suffering Stephen and Sophia.

Finally all had triumphed over the deadly substance.

"So what do you think?" Clint asked Rose hours later, after dinner had been eaten and the kids were tucked in for the night. "Did I win our bet?"

Unable to recall a time when she and her kids had enjoyed more fun, Rose grinned over at him. "You sure did."

He strolled closer, the desire she felt deep inside reflected in his eyes. "We could try orange kryptonite and sweet potato fries the next time they want to play Superheroes."

She'd been hoping he would be game for another round. "Good idea, but…I think you might have to be here for that to be a success."

"That can be arranged." He hooked an arm about her waist and threaded a hand through her hair. Then he kissed her tenderly. "As winner of the bet, I hereby claim our first official date should be this weekend."

"Well, fair is fair, I suppose." Gazing indulgently up at him, she laid her hands on his chest. "The kids are having a sleepover with some of their cousins at my parents' house on Saturday night…"

"Then how about I pick you up here at seven?"

"Sure. Where are we going?"

His smile widened. "Somewhere…surprising."

Chapter Ten

"YOU'VE GOT TO be kidding me." Rose stared at the two horses, saddled and ready, standing patiently in front of her house. As promised, Clint had surprised her for their Saturday evening date.

He lifted his Stetson and resettled it on his head. "You don't like to ride?" Sexy crinkles appeared at the corners of his eyes.

She had spent a long time getting ready herself but was unprepared for how good he looked. The cut of his tan Western sport coat and jeans played up his masculine physique, while the bright white of his shirt contrasted nicely with his sun-bronzed skin and the chestnut strands of his freshly cropped hair. He'd also shaved closely and smelled of leather-and-spice cologne.

"Actually, I love to ride. I just haven't been on a horse in a while. And I'm not sure I'm dressed for it." Rose gestured to the flowered dress and cardigan she had on. "Except, of course, for the boots." She'd pulled on her favorite burgundy cowgirl boots.

He adjusted the brim of his Stetson and smiled down at her. "Silver won't mind if you go as-is."

Nor, apparently, would her date.

Rose thought about changing into jeans, too. She decided against it, given the wardrobe crisis she'd already had, trying to decide what to wear tonight. Her floral sundress with the fitted bodice and full knee-length skirt was long enough to afford her modesty, even in the saddle. The problem would be protecting her bare inner thighs from rubbing against the saddle as she rode.

"Just give me a minute."

She raced back up the stairs. She plucked a pair of rose-colored yoga shorts from her bureau, kicked off her cowgirl boots and shimmied her way into the form-fitting knit.

Satisfied the hem of her dress fell a good four inches beneath the hem of her yoga shorts, she tugged her boots on and raced back down the stairs.

Clint surveyed her head to toe, his gaze lingering on the low neckline of her dress before returning to her eyes. He slid his arm beneath her elbow. "I was hoping you wouldn't change the dress for jeans."

A comment which just confirmed he liked his women feminine. Just as she liked her men big, strong and tall.

She batted her eyelashes at him flirtatiously. "Don't like the way I look in denim?"

He shrugged and watched her move through the downstairs, checking door locks and turning on lights, so it wouldn't be pitch black when they returned. "I wouldn't say that."

She turned sideways. The skirt of her dress brushed him as she passed.

He smiled down at her and fell in step beside her as they walked back to the foyer. "I just like the way you look in this dress." Once again, his hand was on her, this time pressed to the middle of her spine.

She flushed, heating at his light touch, and they hadn't really started their date yet. "Which is what…?"

He leaned down to whisper in her ear. "All soft and womanly."

Rose sucked in a breath. "I probably should tell you that lines like that don't work on me."

"What about this, then?" He used his leverage on her elbow to turn her toward him, then leaned over to kiss her cheek. He drew back just far enough to peer into her eyes. "Does this work?"

More than you know.

Trying not to think how good it felt to be going out with him—even if it was only the payoff to a fun wager—Rose smiled. "Well, cowboy, if we don't get a move on, it'll be dark before we ever get wherever it is we're going." Rose plucked her cowgirl hat from the hat rack next to the door, plopped it on her head, then donned her purse and lacy cardigan sweater as he led the way outside. "Where are we headed?" she asked, locking the door behind her and reveling in the warmth of the late spring evening.

"Another surprise." He slipped his hands around her waist to give her a chivalrous boost up she didn't really need but appreciated just the same. With him still supporting her, she grasped the saddle horn and swung her leg over Silver's back. She settled in the saddle, then tugged the edges of her skirt downward, tucking it modestly around her thighs.

He climbed onto his stallion, and they set off at a leisurely pace, cutting across her property and her neighbors'. Once they were in open terrain, they let their horses pick up the speed. For a while, there was no need for conversation. It was enough just to canter across wildflower-strewn meadows and take in the experience. Eventually they reached one of the two meandering streams on Clint's property. They dismounted and led their horses to the water. Clint had plastic bottles of lemonade in his saddlebag for them.

He offered her a silent toast. Together they drank deeply. Aware she hadn't felt this free or been this relaxed in a long time, Rose leaned against the trunk of a nearby tree. The sun was a golden ball dipping slowly through the pink-streaked sky toward the horizon.

"So this is your idea of the perfect date," she teased.

He came closer. "The Double Creek is one of my favorite places in the world."

Rose could see why. The thousand-acre ranch might be small by some standards, but it was both gorgeous and rugged, with wide-open spaces and moderately rolling terrain. In the distance, they could see the neatly plowed rows that now delineated the acres of blackberry bushes. It was as beautiful and scenic as a Napa Valley vineyard.

She pointed the rim of her bottle toward the fields. "You know, it might be a good idea to film that from here. For the commercial. Up close, you can't really tell how far the crop stretches. The view would be a good sales tool for the berry picker..."

"Let's not talk business tonight," he said in a gently chiding tone.

Heart skittering in her chest, she turned back to face him, wishing he didn't look so damn good. "What do you want to talk about, then?"

He made the face her kids did when confronted with just the thought of ever eating brussels sprouts again, then flashed her a crooked smile. "Anything—everything—else."

She laughed, and he leaned in closer and kissed her. Emotion bubbled up inside her, relentless and undeniable.

Aware her pulse was racing as if he had just made love to her, Rose splayed a hand across his hard chest.

He drew back, his gaze tender. "Hungry?"

For you. Rose nodded, another ribbon of desire curling through her. "I am."

His big hand captured hers, and he pressed a kiss to the back of it. Her insides fluttered.

"Me, too." He grinned, charismatic as ever, then continued huskily, "So what do you say we go on back to my place?"

IT WAS DARK when they reached the stables. Rose helped Clint unsaddle and care for their horses. Once their mounts were given food and water and settled in for the night, the two of them headed up to the Double Creek ranch house.

The aroma of rich and savory beef hit them the moment they walked in the door.

Was this how it felt to have someone take care of you? she wondered. How he felt when he came to her place for dinner?

He smiled at her reaction. Plucked the Western hat off her head, then the Stetson from his, and set both on the hall table along with her purse. Hand beneath her elbow, he steered her toward the kitchen. The breakfast room table had been set—beautifully. A bottle of wine, a loaf of bread and a slow-cooker full of the richest, meatiest-looking beef stew she had ever seen sat on the counter. Rose calculated the effort. "You really went all out," she murmured, impressed.

He tossed her a fond look, then went to wash his hands. "If you only get one date with a lady—" he winked "—you've got to make it count."

Already tingling with anticipation, she joined him at the kitchen sink, taking in the heat and strength and sheer masculinity of him. How was it he always smelled so good? Like fresh air and sunshine. And man. How was it he always made her want him so much?

Deciding it didn't matter as long as they had a reason to keep seeing each other again, she turned to face him, her hip bumping his in the process. "We could always make another bet." In the one-day-at-a-time vein...

He quirked a brow and countered with comically exaggerated seriousness, "But then I'd have to let you *win*."

She let out a low laugh, loving it when he teased her this

way. Like he wanted to capture her heart, as much as she secretly wanted to capture his. "Why?"

Dark eyes twinkling, he lifted his hand to her face and let his thumb rasp gently over her cheekbone to her lower lip. "Because it wouldn't be *fair*, taking advantage of you *two* times in a row."

Already aching for another kiss, she demanded, "Who says I couldn't win on my own?"

"All right." He led her toward the table, held out her chair and waited until she slipped into it. "What do you want to wager?"

Rose watched him put dinner on the table. A serving bowl full of the rich and meaty stew. The bread and butter. A baby lettuce salad, redolent with fresh blackberries, sliced pears and pecans.

"Something about work this time," she suggested, thinking that had to be safer, emotionally, than this. An evening that was beginning to feel all too romantic—and real.

Handing her a bottle of what appeared to be homemade vinaigrette, he groaned in dismay.

"Hey, I haven't said what the payoff is yet!"

He slipped his sport coat over the back of the chair and rolled up his sleeves to just below the elbow. "I'd still prefer it to be about our personal life."

She knew that. She also knew what he could accomplish when he was really and truly motivated.

And given how much he seemed to loathe anything connected with the berry picker, the advertising team, or harvesting...

Wheels turning, she let her gaze roam over his pristine white Western shirt and form-fitting dark denim jeans before lingering on his broad shoulders. His clothes were nice, if unremarkable. But there was nothing ordinary about the body beneath them. He was solid muscle from head to toe. Taut and big and capable in that unutterably masculine way.

Yet capable of great gentleness and tenderness, too.

But it was his brown eyes with the darker rim around the edges that drew her in the most. Made her want to make his life easier, too.

He'd been hurt. Just as she had.

He was wary of making another mistake of the heart, too.

"The sooner the endorsement work gets done," she said, "the quicker you get back to what you really want to be doing—ranching."

Visibly relaxing at the thought of that, he sat down opposite her and handed her a glass of wine. "Good point. All right...you sold me. What's the wager?"

"I bet we can wrap up the filming of the endorsement commercial for the berry picker in just one more week." If they hustled, she knew they could do it, no matter how ridiculous the demands of the Farmtech marketing execs.

"One week?" Abruptly, Clint looked as impatient as she felt. Their eyes met and held for another breath-stealing moment. "I'd like it to be one more day," he lamented with a sigh.

"That's not going to happen, given how slow the advertising team works." Despite how much she wanted to triumph, she couldn't make a sucker bet with him.

He broke the bakery-fresh bread with his hands and heaped stew on both their plates. His usual good humor returned. "All right, then," he conceded, "I'll wager three days."

"That would mean that to win, you would have to cooperate a whole heck of a lot more than you have been thus far," Rose warned.

He shrugged.

"You can't delay or drag things out, either."

"I won't." He leaned toward her, his knees bumping hers beneath the table. "So, if you win…?"

Rose shrugged, ignoring the comforting warmth of his body so close to hers. She did not pull away. Neither, to her delight, did he. "We have a date of my choosing."

Chuckling, he let his gaze rove slowly over her body before returning to her eyes. "Trying to tempt me into deliberately losing our bet?"

Was he that eager to spend time with her? Rose beamed happily at the notion. "No." Tingling everywhere his eyes had touched and everywhere they hadn't, she feigned a serious winner-take-all attitude. "I just want a chance to do things all my way."

The corners of his lips twitched with mirth. "Ah…"

"And if you win?" she asked, shifting back slightly so they were no longer in contact with each other. She was trying very hard to keep this meal on track, lest they end up upstairs in his bed.

"If I triumph," he declared, sliding a hand beneath his roughhewn jaw, matching her solemn tone to the letter, "then I want a dinner with you—and your kids. Done my way."

The shock of his request stole her breath. "Really?" She blinked. "You'd want that?"

Slowly Clint nodded. "The night we all played Superheroes together?" he prodded in a rusty-sounding voice.

She nodded.

"That was one of the best nights of my life."

And best of all, Rose noted happily, he meant it.

CLINT WAS PLEASED to see that Rose was in no hurry to go home, even after dinner was over, dishes done. Instead, she asked for a tour of the barn and the stables—both of which were going to have to be torn down and rebuilt from the ground up—and the first floor of the ranch house, which along with the rest of the sprawling two-story domicile had been completely redone by the previous owner.

"It must have been nice," she remarked as they walked into his newly modernized private study, "to move into a place that was furnished right down to the dishes and linens."

"I didn't mind paying extra for all that." He caught her hand in his. "Others might have balked."

Seemingly content to have her fingers laced with his, she moved over to the long ledge beneath the windows. "What's this?" She pointed to the aerial photographs, new barn and stable blueprints, and survey maps laid out along the two-foot-wide shelf.

Clint did not want to discuss anything that might upset her. Especially given how well the evening had gone so far. Nor did he want to hide what was going to be his future. "Those are the plans for the reconfiguration of the ranch," he told her reluctantly.

She tilted her head, and the gentle movement brought the subtle drift of her sun-warmed perfume. "When did you commission the design?"

"A little over a year ago, when I first bought the ranch," he said. "I just haven't had the time or the money to implement any of the changes I'd like to see yet."

She smiled and locked eyes with him. "So tell me what you want done."

Using his fingertip, he referenced the survey map. "First, separate my ranching operation into two main areas. Put the cattle ranching on the south end. The cutting-horse breeding and training operation to the north. With the ranch house, of course—" he pointed to where they currently stood "—remaining in the middle of the property."

Rose leaned in close to observe, the delicate warmth of her shoulder brushing his in the process. "There's only one problem with that. This line here—" she picked up a pencil to illuminate her point "—where the cattle pastures will be is awfully close to the berry patch." Her soft lips compressed in concern, she pivoted to face him. "Too close, really, since agricultural regulations require a good distance between any livestock and produce operations to prevent cross-contamination."

Clint nodded, more than familiar with state and federal rules. He also had an idea how the evening would end if they continued down this path. There'd be no more laughing and joking around.

No more quiet conversation.

No more getting to know each other the way they needed to if they were to take whatever this was to the next level.

One day soon, of course, they would have to discuss it. But that was not going to be tonight.

He caught her by the wrist and pulled her close. Placing one hand on her waist, weaving the other through her hair, he guided her against him. Softness to hardness. Woman to man.

She gasped, feeling the electric jolt of pure chemistry, too. "Clint…"

He kissed her temple, her brow, the curve of her cheek, the need to make her his stronger than ever. "Enough business. Talking farming and livestock is not why I brought you over here."

"Then why did you?" she asked breathlessly, once again seeming to weigh everything he said and did.

Words weren't always the best way. Sometimes it was better to show someone how you felt. So Clint lowered his mouth to hers. "This."

Rose saw his kiss coming, and though she couldn't avoid it entirely, to his frustration she refused to let it continue beyond the first mesmerizing contact. Hands splayed across the width of his shoulders, she gave him a little shove.

Ever the gentleman, despite himself, he lifted his head. Waited.

She inhaled shakily. "You know there is no future in this," she reminded him.

He kissed the tip of her nose, his thighs still plastered to hers. "I know you think too far ahead."

She jerked in a breath. "Someone has to, because I meant what I said, Clint. I really don't ever want to get married again."

She could say it as much as she wanted. It didn't mean that he was going to believe it. If ever there was a woman crying out for love, it was Rose. He could see it in her eyes and feel it in her kiss. He'd felt it in his chest when he had watched her finally let loose tonight, climb up on Silver and ride. She needed to be free as much as he needed to be connected. They could give each other that in so many ways.

"I've got too much business," Rose rushed on.

He took her hand and led her into the living room. Away from the plans for his future, guaranteed to upset her. "You're right about that." He sank down in a wing chair and tugged her onto his lap.

"Too many responsibilities." Rose shook her head.

Most of which were meant to be shared, in an ideal world anyway.

She linked her arms around his shoulders and looked at him seriously. "But as long as you understand that, and accept that whatever this is between us is only temporary, then we can have this."

We. He liked the sound of that.

"Tonight anyway," she amended quickly.

He wanted a hell of a lot more than that. If she were honest, she would have to admit she did, too. "Is this a challenge?" he murmured, taking in the soft cloud of dark-blond hair around her face. He rubbed the curve of her lips with his thumb. "Because I am very good at meeting challenges."

Lowering her gaze, she traced the pocket on his shirt with her fingertips. "I know that," she whispered.

He cupped her chin and guided it upward until she had no choice but to look into his eyes. "So what's really holding you back?"

She shrugged, her lush breasts rising and falling with each nervous breath. "This house is too big."

For him alone, maybe. With Rose and her kids…well, that would be another story.

"It needs to be filled with a family, Clint." Intuiting the direction of his thoughts, she added resolutely, "One of your own making."

Maybe it was time to put that particular theory to the test. He shifted her off his lap and stood, too. "You want to fix me up with someone?"

The crestfallen look on her face confirmed what he already knew, deep down. She did not want to see him with another woman any more than he wanted to see her with another guy.

"Matchmaking is not really my thing," she hedged.

Talk about an understatement. He tucked a strand of hair behind her ear. "Then what is?"

"Right now? In a very temporary sense, this." She stepped back into his arms, rose on tiptoe, and pressed her breasts against his chest. Her kiss was everything he wanted, lush and evocative, searching, teasing, tempting. Without warning, she'd become the aggressor in a way he found surprising but incredibly sexy nevertheless. Still, he felt like he was taking advantage of her, pretending that all they had, or really could have, between them was sex. Calling on every ounce of self-control he had, he broke off the kiss and took a step back. "Hold it right there, sweetheart. We're not done talking."

Rose stared at him.

She had always known, despite his sometimes grumpy nature, that Clint was gallant to the core. Not that he ever seemed to be cantankerous around anyone but her.

It was like she got under his skin as no one else did, and rubbed him the wrong way. Just like he continuously turned her on. And there was only one cure for the quivering need deep inside her. Only one cure for his own physical need.

"Well, as far as I'm concerned, we are," she returned, as emotional as he was calm. "And you know why? We're only on this date because you won it in a bet! And since we understand this is just a fling, there's no point in examining it too closely."

"Speak for yourself." He took her in his arms and kissed the corner of her mouth. "If we're doing this..." He kissed the other corner.

"Oh, we are," Rose whispered back, unable to help the soft, sultry sound she made in the back of her throat.

Without warning, he scooped her up in his arms and cradled her against his chest. "Then I'm not letting a second of it go without celebrating it the way it deserves."

Excitement roaring through her, Rose wreathed her arms about his neck as he made his way through the first floor, up the stairs and down the hall to the master bedroom. Breathlessly she murmured, "Hey there, cowboy. This is supposed to be a joint venture!" Equal partners, coming together.

He set her down next to his bed. "Uh-huh. Enough of you taking the lead, Rose."

Letting her know with a glance there would be no more negotiating, he reached over and turned on the bedside lamp, illuminating the room in a soft, golden glow. He stepped toward her once again, flashing a sexy grin she found irresistible. "It's my turn to be in charge."

Just that easily, her cardigan was coming off. The zipper on her dress was easing down. His fingers trailed over her spine. Lazily he met her gaze. "Unless you disagree?"

She watched as he guided her dress past her hips, then grinned at his expression when he saw the rose-colored yoga shorts that had protected her sensitive inner thighs from saddle rub. Definitely not what he was expecting, she thought. Although what lay underneath it might be...

"Oh, I think this is fine," Rose said. He knelt before her, helping her out of one cowgirl boot, then the other. Her nipples pearled beneath the lace of her bra.

He regarded her ardently, a sense of purpose glittering in his eyes. "Just fine?" He pressed his face into her lower midriff.

Rose shivered as his thumbs traced the most feminine part of her while his lips made a sensual tour of her bare stomach. A slow, warm heat began to fill her. She closed her eyes, lifting herself to him. "Better than fine."

He peeled off the shorts, then her lace panties, before rising again to reach behind her and relieve her of her bra. "How much better?" he persisted.

Before she could answer, he cupped her face in his hands and kissed her deep and hard, long and slow, his tongue hot and wet and unbearably evocative. Demonstrating just who was in command, he kissed her again until she was lost in the taste and touch and feel of him, lost in the ragged intake of his breath and her own shuddering moan. Yearning welled up inside her until she was his for the taking, and she wanted him, too. So much.

Still kissing him passionately, she tugged his shirt from the waistband of his jeans and jerked open the snaps. That quickly, his magnificent chest was hers to enjoy. He let all he wanted come through in yet another deep, searing kiss, then stepped back, and his eyes on hers, stripped naked, too. Her mouth was dry as he took her hand and lay down with her on the bed.

"A little bit better?" He cupped the soft swells of her breasts in his palms, loving her with his mouth and his lips and his hands.

She shook her head, her whole body turning hot and boneless. "Extraordinarily better."

He rolled over to kiss her, still fulfilling her desires with shocking ease. His hands went to her hips, and he arched slowly against her. Over and over. And still they kissed, while she concentrated on the warmth of his touch and lower still, the urgency of his body.

"What about this?" He slid downward.

She quaked as he found her with his hands, then his lips and tongue. "Oh, ah, that's…nice…too." Shuddering, she caught his head in her hands, willing him never to stop.

She felt him smile against her skin. Unbelievably, he found a way to stroke her even more slowly and erotically. She threw back her head and moaned, and the sound seemed to inspire him even more. "Nice?" he echoed.

She kept her eyes closed as he stroked around, up, in. "Nice is good," she defended herself between jagged breaths. So, so good, as a matter of fact.

He chuckled and shot up to kiss her mouth again. "I was aiming a little higher."

He was sure getting there, she thought, as he found her breasts, the center of his palm rubbing and pressing against the taut tips, while his mouth seared and found solace in hers.

He gripped her hips the way she liked, lifting her and kissing her, until she writhed with passion and moaned for more. "Say, championship-level higher," he muttered playfully.

Once again, he left a trail of kisses over her abdomen to her silky-wet center. He used pressure from within and soft tender exterior strokes until there was only a driving, urgent need. She gasped again, moving against him pliantly. Already sliding toward the edge, she wasn't sure she could take much more. "Your turn," she whispered, wanting to give as well as receive.

He smiled in triumph. "Not necessary."

She took the condom from him, putting it aside—for now. "You'll thank me later." Hand to his chest, she rolled him onto his back.

"I'm thanking you now."

She laughed gently. Hands sliding beneath him, her hair drifting over his spread thighs, she loved him to the very edge. And then loved him some more.

"Not...without you." He tightened his hands on her, urging her upward. Together, they worked on his condom, then shifted so her back was to the mattress. His hard body covered hers, surrounding her with masculine warmth, the feel of him pressed up against her giving her a whole-body shiver.

He kissed her again, long and lingeringly. Drawing out the moment, celebrating the occasion, just the way he had said they would. Their eyes met. They were really doing this. Again. And foolish or not, Rose realized, she wanted him with all her heart and soul.

Breathing roughly, he parted her thighs with his knee. She surrendered completely, opening herself up to him as she wrapped her arms and legs around him. More kisses followed. With a whisper of her name and a groan, he finally slid home.

Magic happened. He took; she gave. Then she took and he gave. And suddenly, there was no more waiting. No more wondering. Just the sudden opening of her heart and the fire and passion of their joining. He made love to her as if nothing else in the world mattered. And, Rose realized, feeling more deliriously happy than she ever had in her life, for that brief time, nothing else did.

Chapter Eleven

"I guess it's my turn now," Clint teased her long moments later.

Rose's breathing had finally gone back to normal, but the rest of her was still all riled up. As if sensing the commotion going on deep inside her, Clint rolled onto his side, taking her with him. Arms still clasped warmly around her, he waited until she met his eyes.

His sexy-gruff demeanor had her relaxing, despite her post-lovemaking jitters. "*Your* turn? For what?" she asked, making no effort to disguise her confusion.

He rubbed the moisture from his lips with the pad of his thumb. "To say that this wasn't exactly how I envisioned the evening going."

A reference to her remarks after the first time they'd made love…

"There wasn't going to be any lovemaking tonight," he continued even more tenderly.

What was it they said about best laid plans…? She cuddled closer, loving the way he used that enticing mixture of humor and gallantry to soothe her worries away. "I guess we blew that objective, huh?"

"Definitely." He stroked a hand through her hair. "Tonight was supposed to be about romance."

She luxuriated in the feel of his hands on her skin. "Making love is romantic."

"And the fun part of getting to know each other," he concurred, kissing the top of her head.

Rose sighed blissfully. She could feel the strong steady beat of his heart beneath her cheek. "The aftermath is fun, too."

And, if you discounted the time she spent with her family, she hadn't had a lot of fun in her life lately.

Clint shifted so he was lying beside her, his head propped on his upturned hand. Looking as sexually content as she felt, he continued, "The point is, I wanted you to know I'm interested in a lot more than just taking you to bed."

Rose sat up against the headboard, the sheet drawn up over her breasts. "Which is a problem in and of itself."

He sat up, too. "Why?"

"Because I've already explained we're all wrong for each other in the long run," she said as gently as she could.

A brief silence fell. "So you weren't just playing hard to get." Hurt and disappointment flashed in his eyes. "You really don't want to get any closer."

Resisting the urge to get up and run out before things got any more complicated, Rose reached behind her to fluff and adjust the pillows. They were both grown-ups. There was no reason for her to behave in a cowardly manner. "It's a lot deeper than that."

He let out a sharp breath. "I'm listening."

The problem was, she didn't know quite how to say it so a fiercely proud man like Clint would accept it. All she knew for certain was that it was hard enough just trying to stay friends and limited business partners with a man like Clint.

If they talked too much—or she thought too much—she'd start daydreaming up all the reasons why she and

Clint should be together. She'd start imagining him in her life, and herself in his. Before she knew it, those dreams would include her triplets, and maybe even kids of their own. And that was completely crazy, too.

She knew how detrimental it was on a marriage to raise multiples, and that the divorce rate for people who married for a second time was a staggering 50 percent. Put those statistics together, and the odds were stacked against her of realistically making another marriage work over the long haul, or at least until her kids were grown and completely out on their own. And that was going to be another eighteen years from now.

Time in which Clint should be marrying for love and starting his own biological family.

But, knowing he was unlikely to accept that argument, she met his probing gaze and recited another sobering statistic. "You know multiples run in my family."

He trailed his fingertips from her shoulder to elbow, eliciting evocative tingles wherever he brushed. "And that is important right now because…?" He bent his head and pressed a kiss to her wrist.

She brought her knees up between them, like a shield. "I can't have another baby, Clint." *Not even with you.*

Watching his brow furrow, she wrapped her arms around her knees and pressed on, "Because if I got pregnant again, I might have another two or three all at once, instead of just the one." *Just like before.*

She recalled the stricken look on Barry's face when he heard they were having multiples. The completely overwhelmed way he had acted.

She couldn't bear the thought of ever seeing Clint look at her that way. Another tsunami-like wave of anxiety shifted over her. "And that's another reason why you and I can't even—" *think about having any kind of future.* Because it wouldn't be fair to deprive him of the magical experience of having his own baby.

"Slow down, now." Clint sat up against the headboard, too, and gathered her in his arms. Holding her close, he stroked a hand through her hair. "That's not the kind of thing I can run statistics on in my head, Rose, but I think the odds of you having another set of multiples are pretty small."

Her throat tightened. "Don't forget, my parents had twins and triplets."

"And one single birth, too."

True. They'd had Poppy...

Rose let her head drop to the comforting curve of Clint's shoulder. Closing her eyes, she let herself curl into the soothing ministrations of his massaging palm.

"Furthermore—" the sexy rumble was back in his voice "—I wouldn't mind if you and I did have multiples together."

Which was what Barry had said to everyone right up until the time he had told her the truth—that it was too much—and left her, when the triplets were three months old.

Rose pushed her unease away. "Well, there's no need to worry about that. I went on the pill after I had the kids, and I've stayed on it to regulate my hormones. So between that and the condoms we've used, we're doubly protected." They would not have to worry about an unexpected pregnancy.

He shifted her over onto his lap. The sheet was twisted between them, but she could still feel the depth of his desire for her. "You're determined to keep this as unsentimental as possible, aren't you?"

The tips of her breasts pearled. Lower still, there was an enormous amount of heat. She released a shuddering breath. "I just want us both to know where we stand."

"Oh, I think we do." He kissed her deeply.

She clung to him, aware she hadn't yet figured out what all of this meant or would ever come to mean. "Clint…"

"We don't have to decide everything tonight, sweetheart. All we have to do right now is focus on what we feel in this moment."

And what he seemed to want, Rose realized as he made love to her all over again, was to be in the here and now. And that, she found, she could do.

SUNDAY CAME ALL too soon, and with it, dinner with the entire family. "These are, without a doubt, the most magnificent blackberries I have ever tasted," Rose's mom said.

"I agree," her dad chimed in.

Rose smiled at her parents. "Thanks."

"Too bad it's the last year for them," Gannon put in.

Rose arched a brow at her brother-in-law. "What do you mean?"

He shrugged. "Clint is going to mow them down."

"I know that was the plan," Rose said. "But that was before he saw how much money he could make from them."

Gannon nodded and said nothing more, but her sisters and her parents exchanged worried glances.

"How close are you and Clint?" her mom, Lacey, asked later as the two of them loaded the dishwasher.

All the other adults were outside, supervising the kids.

"What do you mean?" Rose asked, stalling.

Her mom put the leftover blackberry pie in the fridge. "Are you dating him?"

Rose shrugged and worked on cleaning the counters. "We went riding—" *and had dinner and made love repeatedly* "—last night as payoff for a bet he won. That's it."

"It doesn't look quite as simple as that."

Rose felt herself flush. "Mom…"

Lacey touched her shoulder. "Just be careful, honey. I know how vulnerable you are, deep down."

Rose dried the pans and then handed them over to her mom to hang on the overhead pot rack. "And how I tend to rush into things?"

"You've only done that once before, with Barry."

Rose jerked in a breath. "And it was a disaster."

Lacey waved off the mistake. Gently she said, "The two of you just weren't right for each other, that's all. You didn't want the same things out of life."

The question was, did she and Clint?

Rose was still pondering the matter the next morning when she arrived at the Double Creek. She wasn't surprised to see the advertising team and film crew already there. They'd been gung ho about crafting this next section of the advertising campaign. Clint looked less pleased.

As before, there were also a half-dozen farm-equipment execs and several members of the local sales center, including Jeff.

Rose wasted no time in joining them. "How's it going, fellas?" she asked cheerfully.

Aaron Diehl, the marketing director of Farmtech, said, "We were just telling Clint that while the footage we already shot of him driving the berry picker is fine, it doesn't give us what we need. We have to figure out a way to make it look sexy."

Clint shook his head in frustration. "I've been telling them there's no way to do it."

He was right.

"There's a lot to love about the berry picker," Rose agreed, "but it's not sexy. Clint, on the other hand, is."

Suddenly everyone was listening to what she had to say.

Aware she was on a roll, Rose continued, "You hired him because he's a rodeo star and a rancher, so why not use that? Why not shoot some film of him riding around his ranch on his horse? He has a beautiful stallion."

And Clint looked amazing in the saddle. Masculine and strong, all alpha male. Inspired by their previous evening together, she went on, "You could also use footage from his rodeo days, in the cutting-horse competition. Tie the champion he was then to the champion he has in the berry picker or whatever." She waved an airy hand. "I don't know. It's not really my field of expertise, but..."

Ted beamed. "I like it."

"So do I," Jeff put in.

So did everyone else.

Except Clint, who reacted with a grimace, but appeared to go along with it reluctantly, nevertheless.

"Then let's get to it," the director of the commercial campaign said.

While Clint was off with the team, Rose took over the driving of the berry picker. It was more fun than she had imagined. Easier, too.

By the time Clint was finished, hours later, she had brought in the day's haul. Volunteers from the co-op had taken the crates of fruit and loaded them into the refrigerated truck.

"You want me to go with Swifty to Rose Hill Farm and get the fruit all put away?" Mary Beth Simmons asked.

Rose smiled at her good friend. The local PTA president had a knack for always being where she was needed and quickly taking charge. "I'd really appreciate it." She handed Mary Beth the keys to the barn.

"No problem." The young woman waved at Swifty and then headed off.

Clint joined her a moment later. Trying not to notice how handsome he looked with his skin bronzed from the spring sun, Rose gazed up at him. "How did it go?"

He swept his hat off and came closer, inundating her

with the intoxicating smells of soap and leather. "I didn't fall off my horse, if that's what you're asking."

Rose turned her eyes away from the plaid Western shirt that covering his broad shoulders and the tan leather chaps he'd put on over his dark-blue jeans. She'd heard they'd had him riding horseback through heavy brush on some of the still neglected areas of the Double Creek.

She could only imagine how sexy those shots had been, given his dark, brooding mood. After all, he had not exactly been thrilled with the whole idea of being used as eye candy.

"It's almost over," she said soothingly.

He frowned. "I wish."

She was about to ask what he meant by that when she was joined again by the director of the ad team filming the commercial as well as several other execs. "We'd hoped to get at least part of the interview with Clint on the front porch of his ranch house, on film today."

Obviously it hadn't happened.

Clint's eyes never left hers. "Did you know about this?" he asked brusquely. "That they planned to use my *home* in the commercials?"

Without specifically asking him.

Bad enough they were doing this on his ranch, Rose knew. He'd accepted that because it was the only way to bring in the crop.

Opening up his private domain to the public at large was another matter entirely.

Understanding this was an unwanted turn of events and an invasion of his privacy, she shook her head. "We could do it at my home, if you like," she offered. Although it would slow down the process considerably. Something Clint was unlikely to tolerate well, either.

Clint winced—her idea no more acceptable than the first. In a voice dripping with sarcasm, he asked, "How about I just stand next to the berry picker instead? Out in the field somewhere?"

Everyone on the team looked at Rose, again expecting her to do something to calm the "talent" and sweet-talk him into cooperating fully.

As pleasantly as possible, Rose said, "I think it will be easier and more comfortable for everyone this way, Clint." Especially since the porch had already been staged, the lighting and cameras set up.

"Fine," Clint said brusquely. "Let's just get it over with."

Make-up was called in once again. Sound and lighting checks followed. Finally, Clint was seated in one of his rustic wooden armchairs. Aware their star was about to implode, Rose lingered in the foreground, watching.

"So how has the berry picker made your life better?" the interviewer, a pretty blonde in Western clothing, asked Clint.

Looking stymied, he lifted his hands. "It really hasn't."

She tried again. "Was the berry picker easy to use?"

He shrugged. "If you can drive a tractor, you can drive a berry picker."

Good, Rose thought. Finally, a question and answer on tape they could use.

The reporter looked at the questions. "How has it affected your daily yield?"

He paused. Lifted an aimless hand, then let it fall back on the arm of the chair. "Haven't a clue. I never brought in a crop before."

The interviewer leaned toward him. "It must greatly automate the process."

"To some degree, I guess. But you still need workers who can lift the crates of fruit on and off the bed of the machine, so it's not like—"

"Cut!" Aaron yelled.

Clint shot him a questioning look. "What did I say?"

"You have to sell this thing."

"That's the problem." Clint grimaced. "I don't *want* to sell this thing!"

"Can I have a moment with Clint?" Rose led him aside so they could speak privately. Aware everyone was watching, she whispered, "I thought you wanted to get this completely wrapped up in three days."

His jaw hardened. "I do."

"Well, the way things are going, it will take at least a week."

He drew in a long breath. Exhaled. She ran her palm over the swell of his biceps, consoling him as best she could under the circumstances. "Can you at least try and cooperate?" she asked patiently.

He cast a peeved look at their audience. "I am."

"But—?"

"I don't know anything about farming. You can ask me about ranching. I'll be glad to tell them anything and everything I've learned, but if you want me to talk about the beauty of mechanized berry pickers and growing fruit, you're going to have to do what we discussed previously and give me something to memorize."

He had a point. A "candid" interview had not been part of the original proposal. It was unfair to expect Clint to talk knowledgably about something he had no expertise in.

Rose went back to talk to the others. As soon as a solution was negotiated, she went back to Clint, who looked no happier to be standing around now than he had earlier.

"They're calling it a day," she reported.

Clint nodded in relief. Although he'd been closely shaven when they had their date, he hadn't bothered since. The two-day stubble gave him a sexy, don't-mess-with-me look she found almost as enticing as his lonesome-cowboy attitude.

If ever there was a man crying out for taming...

Telling herself this was neither the time nor the place

to indulge in tantalizing fantasies, she continued in the same businesslike tone, "They'll be back bright and early tomorrow to pick up where we left off today."

"Filming on the porch?"

"Except this time the ad team is going to write a script for you and put it on cue cards for you to read."

He looked as thrilled about that as Rose had expected him to be. Feeling a little like a talent wrangler, she continued sternly, "You're also going to get tutored by me."

He ran his hand beneath his jaw. "In reading cue cards?"

Rose kept her gaze away from his delectably full lower lip. "Funny. No, in everything you ever wanted or needed to know about blackberries, and the growing and harvesting of them, but were afraid to ask."

He shrugged his broad shoulders. "Sounds…sexy."

"You wish." She warned him with a glance not to get any ideas. "We're going to be very well-chaperoned by my little ones."

He chuckled as if looking forward to spending time with all four of them. "Sounds even more fun."

The hell of it was, she knew he meant it. If he didn't deserve to have biological children of his own…

But he did.

So she couldn't go there.

"You're welcome to join us for dinner if you want," she said, glancing at her watch.

His grin widened as if he'd just won another championship trophy. "What should I bring?"

"Just yourself," she countered, not liking the ornery gleam in his eyes one bit. The one that said he'd be kissing her again before the night was over. "And a better attitude."

CLINT ARRIVED TO find all three triplets sitting on the front porch, glum looks on their faces, their chins in their hands. "What's going on?"

Sophia confessed, "We're in time-out."

He sat on the steps beneath them. "How come?"

Scarlet sighed. "We were fighting again."

"I did not want to play husband," Stephen explained. "I'm tired of being married!"

Scarlet put her hands on her hips. "Well, I'm not!"

Clint turned to the shyest. "Sophia?"

She frowned. "I think I'm like Mommy. I don't want to get married. But I do like playing baby dolls. And house."

"What about you?" Stephen peered at Clint suspiciously. "Do you want to be a husband?"

Clint nodded, not ashamed to admit, "I do. Now." *Now that I've met Rose. And made love with her. And had a glimpse of how perfect our lives could be.* "When I was your age, not so much."

Clint thought about a way to achieve peace here, as Rose had done earlier at his ranch. "Maybe we could all play Superheroes again."

Three more scowls appeared. "Mommy says we're not allowed because we were fighting," Scarlet explained. "We have to get along and then we get an award."

"Reward," Clint corrected her.

Stephen blinked. "What's that?"

Clint was about to answer when the screen door opened. Rose stepped out. She was dressed in a scoop-neck sky-blue T-shirt with three-quarter sleeves, a pair of white shorts, and flip-flops that showed off her pretty painted toenails. The sight of all that soft silky leg nearly had him on his knees.

Rose looked at Clint in surprise. "I didn't know you were here."

Throat dry, he managed, "Just arrived."

But maybe he should have been here sooner.

She looked harried. For the first time, he realized what a long day it had been for her. How hard she was working on his behalf as well as her own. He felt guilty for not be-having better, trying harder with the advertising team. So what if the deal with Farmtech wasn't what he wanted? It was what *she* wanted. Plus, financially, once it was all said and done, it would assist them both monetarily. At least for this year, while the blackberries were still on his property.

Deciding to help in the best way he knew how, he asked, "Got any storybooks?"

She blinked.

"I was thinking maybe I could read to the kids while you finish up in there. Unless there is something else you'd rather we all do?"

She shook off the cobwebs. Began to smile. "No. Read-ing is fine. Reading is good, actually. You-all just sit right there and I'll bring some books."

He appreciated the view of her very nice backside as she disappeared into the house.

"You're really going to read to us?" Sophia asked.

He accepted hugs from all three kids. "I sure am."

"Then we have to go inside, because when we read sto-ries, we read them on the sofa!" Scarlet said.

They looked so excited at the prospect, Clint got a lit-tle choked up at the thought of what a daddy-like thing it was to do.

Sophia clung to his hand. "None of mommy's boy-friends ever read-ed to us before."

Clint knew. It was a damn shame. They'd been fools, all three of them.

Stephen squinted. "Are you Mommy's boyfriend, Mr. Clint?"

"Uhh...no, I'm not." *Technically.*

All three kids gawked at him. Finally Scarlet asked, "Then how come Mommy told Aunt Lily you might be?"

Chapter Twelve

Hours later, when the triplets were finally in bed for the night, Clint saw his chance.

He sauntered into the kitchen, letting his gaze drift slowly over Rose as he noted yet again how unbelievably pretty she looked this evening. "So…" He took up a place at the counter, determined to give her a hard time. The kind he would have given her had they dated back in high school. "You've been talking about me."

Rose looked up so suddenly, she nearly dropped the bowl of luscious ripe blackberries in her hand. "How do you know that?" She set it on the counter, then went back to the fridge and returned with two more bowls. "I mean," she corrected herself hastily, guilty color sweeping her cheeks, "with whom have I been conversing?"

He folded his arms over his chest. "Ah. So there's more than one audience?"

She couldn't contain a laugh. "I don't know what to say to that. At all."

He noticed she wasn't denying it.

It was comforting to realize she spent as much time pondering him as he did her. He moved close enough to drink in the citrus of her perfume. "I am referencing what you said to Lily about me possibly being your boyfriend."

Another small, slight start. Enough to let him know he'd hit the nail on the head.

Averting her gaze, she motioned for him to take a seat at the kitchen island. "We're a little old for that, don't you think?"

He settled in on a stool and watched the hem of her shorts ride higher on her thighs as she did the same. "It does sound a little high school." He swiveled so they were facing each other, their knees touching. "Then again," he drawled, savoring the heat of her bare skin through his jeans, "what we've been doing—sneaking around, stealing kisses—is a little high school, too."

He wagged his brows and leaned toward her.

She cut off his pass with a hand plastered on the center of his chest. She seemed to know, as did he, that if they started making out, they'd never get around to the scheduled tutorial.

"You're here for a reason tonight, cowboy," she warned him with mock sternness, "and this isn't it."

He heaved a huge sigh of disappointment. "So I guess our, ah, *schooling* will be limited to blackberry crops tonight." Which was too bad, given how much they could still learn about each other in other, more provocative ways…

Briefly Rose looked disappointed about that, too. But, as always, she was quick to get back on task. "Yes. But before you get that surly look on your face, I think you're going to like it." She dragged the three bowls in different colors toward him. "I want you to taste all of these and tell me which blackberries you like best."

That was easy. "The ones from the blue bowl."

She raised her brows. "What was wrong with the other two?"

"Nothing." Clint shrugged. "They were just a little bland."

She sat up straight, the new posture emphasizing the

fullness of her breasts. Between that and her bare thighs, he had a hard time concentrating on what she was saying. "Guess where the ones from the blue bowl came from?"

Clint shifted his gaze to her face. "The Double Creek."

Rose beamed. "Exactly! Guess where the others came from?"

His gaze tracked the elegant column of her throat down to the second undone button of her shirt. "No idea."

Unaware of how the soft, silky texture of her skin drove him crazy, she said, "The yellow-bowl berries are from a farm outside San Angelo."

"Okay." Come to think of it, so did her lips...

"Can you tell the difference?"

In you and every other woman on the planet? Hell, yeah! Aware she was expecting an answer, he nodded as scientifically as possible, adding, "I could taste it."

"Do you know what the difference is?"

Between you and other women? Yes. You are amazingly ambitious and inventive and loving and tender and practical and romantic and idealistic and sexy, God, so damn sexy...

"Clint!"

Time to get back on track again. He shook his head, forcing himself to consider the blackberries. "To tell you the truth, they all look exactly the same to me. Except... maybe the ones from my ranch are a little bigger and juicier."

"And yet they are the very same type of Brazos blackberry."

O-kay. "So what is the difference?" he asked in return, curious now. What made the darn blackberries on his ranch so special that everyone raved about them, to the point that he felt guilty for even thinking about mowing them all down?

"The makeup of the soil, how long they went without

being picked, the amount of rain and sun the bushes get. It all plays a part in the final product, and there is no way to duplicate it exactly. Meaning you can't just pick up one hundred acres of berry bushes and move them to another location."

They would see about that. Or something equivalent, anyway. "Surely you could take cuttings or seeds from these particular plants and start them elsewhere," he said.

"Yes. You can. And by the way, my cousin's wife, Amy Carrigan-McCabe, is interested in doing just that for her greenhouses. You should call her and see what the two of you can work out." She huffed out a breath. "But even if you do, there's still no guarantee that if these plants grow elsewhere, the crop will turn out to be the same."

Clint grimaced. "Is this a tutoring session or a sales pitch?" One thing was for sure: it was reminding him of his hard-charging ex, the way she had constantly pressured him to do what *she* wanted without considering what was right for him in the long run. Rose paused. "I'm pushing a little too hard, aren't I?"

Clint saw no reason to lie. "You think?" Taking advantage of Rose's earlier admonition to make himself at home, he got up and helped himself to a glass of water. She rose, too, went to the fridge, and brought out two bottles of cold beer. She handed him one. Even better. "At least tell me you are considering keeping these bushes," she said.

He worked off the bottle cap. "Rose…"

She struggled with her own. "Tell me you wouldn't just destroy the fields without talking to me first."

He took the bottle and twisted the cap off for her. "Of course I would tell you."

Her shoulders slumped slightly in relief.

He held the ice-cold beer against his chest. "That's not the same as asking for your permission." He looked at her long enough to make his feelings clear. "Or negotiating a happy medium, as you are prone to do, because I've already done that with you in agreeing to test and promote the berry picker, and let your business sell and distribute the current crop."

Brought up short by his summation, she sipped her beer. "That's true. You have."

Clint knew he'd made his point, that she accepted the truth of everything he had just said. Yet he still had the sense she hadn't really given up and, like his ex, might not ever forgive him if he didn't eventually do exactly as she wanted.

Irritated to find himself in the same situation that had caused his only other really serious relationship to go bust, Clint took another sip, then put the bottle down on the counter. "Listen, it's been a long day…"

Her eyes widened with shock and hurt. "You're leaving?"

He nodded, knowing it was for the best, for both of them. "I've got some thinking to do."

He thanked her for dinner, the berries, the tutorial and the beer. And headed on home.

IT WAS AMAZING, Rose thought the next day, still stinging a little from Clint's abrupt departure from her home the previous evening. Amazing how he could read so eloquently and beautifully to her three children, yet couldn't recite the most simple sentences off the cue cards. Never mind imbue them with any sort of authenticity! If she didn't know better, she would think he was doing it on purpose!

"Are you still trying to get fired?" she asked him accusingly on the first break of the morning.

Because if so, that wasn't cool.

They had two more weeks, minimum, of berries to harvest, and she didn't want the farm equipment company pulling the machine away. Which, she figured, given the poor effort Clint was making, they had every right to do.

"I don't know what you're talking about," he muttered.

Rose gave him a skeptical look. Clearly he was working some sort of agenda, and she was determined to get to the bottom of it. Hand beneath his elbow, she guided him well out of earshot of everyone else.

"Come on, Clint. What's really going on here? Are you trying to get them to take their berry picker and find someone else who will be a whole lot more cooperative?"

He regarded her impassively. "That's not what I want at all."

When she looked into his eyes, she could almost believe him. *Almost* being the operative word.

He shrugged, continuing, "All I ever had to do when I endorsed the other two products was smile for the camera. There was no acting involved, which was good, because I'm *not* an actor."

He wasn't the only one losing patience. "But you are a reasonably intelligent human being."

Dark brows arching, he echoed, "Reasonably?"

Refusing to let the depth of his sarcasm chase her off, Rose lifted her chin and geared up for battle. "Given the way I'm feeling right now about your performance, that is a charitable description."

This was the point where she half expected him to ask her whose side she was on. Instead, he studied her a very long moment. Then went absolutely still, until he finally nodded and said, "Okay, Rose. Why don't you show me how it should be done?"

Why did she think this was a trick question?

"Really. You're so on top of things," he continued as an audience began to gather around them. He waved his finger emphatically. "Why don't *you* demonstrate?"

If he was going to throw down the gauntlet, she was

damn well going to pick it up. "Fine!" Rose fumed. "I will. And in doing so, I will show you it's not that difficult to read a cue card, cowboy."

Rose gallivanted up the steps and took a seat on the chair they'd set up for him. She looked right into the camera, smiled with every ounce of conviction she had, and then recited the paragraph of promotion material she had memorized the first time he'd had to say it. When she finished, the crew clapped, hooted and hollered.

She stood, glaring at Clint. "See? Not so hard at all."

The director lifted a hand before she could step off the porch. "Say it again. Maybe if you demonstrate it a couple of more times for Clint, it will sink in."

So Rose did, each time getting a little better than the last. Mostly because it was so darn easy.

"Maybe she should pretend to answer a few questions about the machine, too," Ted added. "After all, she drove the berry picker all day yesterday. It's not like she doesn't know how it works."

Glances were exchanged. Aaron asked, "How about it, Rose? Are you game?"

Rose smiled. "Sure."

So they asked. Rose answered. "Would you recommend it to your fellow farmers?"

"Absolutely!" Rose said, the words pouring straight from her heart. "I mean, without the Farmtech berry picker there was no way to get this crop harvested."

Another round of applause was followed by even more compliments on her performance. At the end, Ted nodded toward Clint, who was off talking to one of the crew members about what to look for when buying a horse. "Think you could work with him? Get him to learn the lines?" Ted asked her.

Rose nodded. "I know I can." She turned to Clint, who

was now walking up to join them. "Want to come to my place again for dinner?" she asked him.

His eyes lighting up with an enthusiasm that had been missing that day, Clint nodded. "Sure," he said.

"Then we'll give you this evening to manage it, and try again tomorrow," Ted promised.

Which was coincidentally the last day of her bet with Clint, Rose thought. If Clint won, that was.

And she was pretty sure he still wanted to do that, if only because he was a natural-born competitor and athlete at heart.

Unless... Was it possible he was trying to draw this out on purpose so they could spend more time together?

While the romantic part of Rose wouldn't have minded so much if that were the case, the business side of her knew any inefficiency on their part was not good.

She would have to make Clint understand that.

AT ROSE'S SUGGESTION, Clint spent what was left of his morning working with his cattle and horses over at Gannon's ranch.

The ad team labored under Rose's supervision at the Double Creek, filming the berry fields from different angles and distances.

Rose texted him that from there, she and the team went to Rose Hill Farm to get some footage of the berries being unloaded from the refrigerated truck and set out for sale in the co-op. They also taped testimonials from customers there to purchase the berries.

Relieved to see his secret plan going even better than he had hoped, Clint hit the shower. And headed to her place, as promised, at six o'clock.

Once again, the triplets were sitting on the front porch of the bungalow, waiting for his arrival. They raced to greet him as soon as he stepped out of his pickup truck. Enjoying the mass exuberance, he scooped all three of them up in his arms and gave them a great big group hug.

"Mr. Clint, you are *so strong*!" Sophia observed.

"And you-all are *so cute*!" He set them gently down on the ground. "And your mommy is *so cute*, too."

The triplets giggled. "Isn't he *strong*, Mommy?"

"And *cute*, too." She winked, appearing happier than he would have expected her to be with him, given his really lame performance that morning.

She gazed at the kids. "Did you ask him yet?"

Scarlet took charge. "We got a new game. Want to play?"

He shrugged, affable. "Sure."

"I don't know." Rose shook her head in mock skepticism. "It's a tough one. Sure you are up for it, Mr. Clint?"

He was up for anything with her. Didn't she know that? He telegraphed his sentiments with a look. "I'll give it my best try."

She gave him a wry look, meaning that was more than he had done earlier in the day. Finally, the reaction he had been expecting from her. He fought off a flash of guilt.

Rose was right to think he had screwed up on purpose. But his shenanigans were for the greater good. Eventually everyone would realize that.

"So what is it?" He returned his attention to the aforementioned game.

"Guess!" Stephen bounced up and down, then climbed the post on the porch like a monkey.

Clint wrapped his arms around the little tyke's waist and lifted him down before he hurt himself. "Ah, okay. Is it checkers?"

"No." Sophia lost her shyness long enough to shout. "That's the game! Guess!"

"Guess What This Is!" Rose explained. With a crook of her finger, she led the way inside. Four stools had been pulled up at the kitchen island, and she asked everyone to take a seat.

"We're wearing blin'folds on our eyes!" Stephen explained, so enthusiastic he could barely sit still in his chair.

"Sounds exciting," Clint said. So exciting he wouldn't mind doing that with Rose at another time.

Rose clearly tried not to react to the suggestive look he gave her but blushed faintly just the same.

He grinned.

She flushed some more.

Averting her glance from his, she stepped behind each contestant and tied on the red bandanas one by one. "Okay now, everybody, can you see anything?"

"Noooooo!"

"Great. Here's the tricky part." Rose enunciated carefully, taking the time to make sure the kids comprehended the instructions. "I'm going to hand you-all a stick of something at the same time." She held up her index finger. "You get *one* bite."

"Can't we have *two* bites?" Scarlet asked, as ready to argue as ever.

"All right," Rose relented.

Clint could hear the smile in her voice.

"Two. And then when I ask you what it is, you have to shout out the answer at the same time. You're going to have five chances, or five different things to taste. If you can guess at least three of them right, you win a prize, which you will get at the end. Okay. Everybody ready?"

"Yes!" the four contestants said in unison.

"The first one is easy," Rose said. "What do you think it is?"

"Carrot!" the triplets shouted in unison.

"Eggplant!" Clint crowed.

Everyone laughed.

"The kids got it right, but that's okay, Mr. Clint," Rose

soothed in a voice that said it wasn't the end of the world after all. "Maybe you'll get it next time."

The next round started.

"Green bean!" the kids shouted while Clint yelled, "Asparagus!"

"I'm sure you'll get the next one," Rose predicted cheerfully.

And Clint did. As did everyone else. It was a pretzel stick.

The fourth was a cucumber. Which everyone got.

The fifth, slivers of beefsteak tomato.

"Wow," Rose said when the bandanas came off. She looked at her children admiringly. "You-all did really well tonight." She brought five orange ice pops out of the freezer and handed them out. The kids went out back to eat theirs. Clint and Rose stayed behind for the clean-up.

"Nice job," he said, admiring how pretty she looked in the dusky light. "Getting them to eat their vegetables without really eating their vegetables in the traditional sense."

"I decided to take a page from your book, stop making it all business and have a little fun with the situation instead. A fact that led me straight to the solution."

"In any case, well done." He leaned forward, his lips hovering over hers, wanting to do what he had hoped to do all day.

The door slammed.

"Mommy!" Stephen exclaimed, his tone strident. "Are you and Mr. Clint *kissing*?"

WE WERE ABOUT TO, Rose thought on a wistful sigh. Beside her, Clint merely smiled. "What would you think if that were the case?" Clint asked as the two girls joined their brother.

"Yuck!" Stephen wrinkled his nose.

"It's not yuck!" Scarlet immediately disagreed. "It's romantic! Like in our aunts' weddings."

"Did you see the videos?" Sophia asked. "Mommy doesn't have one, but Aunt Maggie and Aunt Callie and Aunt Lily all do."

Scarlet corrected, "Aunt Poppy and Aunt Violet don't have them."

Clint gave Rose a look. He seemed to be wondering why that was such a hot topic of conversation.

Reluctantly Rose explained, "We've been viewing wedding videos to help Poppy with her private adoption application. The agency wants video of Poppy and Trace Caulder—"

"They actually got together?" Clint interrupted in surprise.

"In a way. It's a long story." An adult story. One that involved two friends who sometimes slept together and were probably in love with each other, but too stubborn and stuck in their own divergent life-paths to admit it. "I'll tell you later."

"Looking forward to it," Clint returned in that low, sexy voice she loved.

"Is dinner ready, Mommy?" Stephen chimed in. "We're still hungry."

"Yes. It is. You-all go wash up, and Mr. Clint and I will get it on the table."

As soon as the kids headed for the bathroom upstairs, Clint hooked his hand around her waist and pulled her against him, hip to hip and chest to chest. He leaned in close, his warm breath fanning against her cheek.

Gazing up at him, a thrill shot through her, along with ever-deepening desire.

He tucked a strand of hair behind her ear. "Do you have any idea how much I missed you last night?"

"I believe so…" A mixture of longing and contentment melted her insides. "And I missed you, too," she whispered.

This time, he did kiss her in a way that felt like a down payment to their future.

"So what's the deal with the wedding videos again?" Clint asked Rose later, when the kids had gone off to bed.

As always when the subject of matrimony was brought up, she turned evasive. Like she didn't want to think about it. But she answered him anyway. "Poppy and Trace have no plans to get married. They just want to adopt together. The private agency they are using feels they will have a better chance of pairing Poppy and Trace with an expectant mom if they can demonstrate how great they are together. And with Trace overseas with the Air Force, these videos are really all they've got."

She took two bottles of sparkling water from the fridge and handed him one. "But weddings are such joyful occasions, and everyone is so happy, it's a good event to show people. The birth mother will see not just Poppy and Trace but also the extended family the child will have."

He followed her into the family room and settled next to her on the sofa, where she'd already laid out the information they were supposed to be studying together that evening. "You're not looking at your wedding?" he asked.

She'd barely sat down before she jumped back up again. "I didn't have one," she called over her shoulder. "Barry and I eloped."

He watched her bend over to root around in the pantry. It was a nice view. Very nice, as a matter of fact. "How come?"

She came back carrying a bag of cheese curls. "A lot of reasons." She tugged at the bag with both hands and ripped it open. "My parents weren't gung ho about us getting married when we did. His parents were divorced and not speaking—at all. So trying to bring all that together would have been a nightmare." She munched on a cheese curl. "We ran off to Vegas instead."

He studied the turbulent emotion in her eyes. "Did you ever regret not having a family ceremony like your sisters?"

She shrugged and offered him the bag. "It would have been nice to have all our family and friends there wishing us well."

A little surprised to see her chowing down on junk food, but enjoying this side of her as much as any other, he accepted her offer. The cheese curls were, as he had expected, crunchy, salty and delicious. And of no nutritional value whatsoever. Which made them even more of a guilty pleasure.

Wondering if it was the talk of anything related to marriage stressing her out, or just him in general, he tested her reaction further. "And think of the other things you missed out on. The dress…"

She suppressed a smile.

"The veil…"

She licked the cheesy residue off her fingers. "The groom in fancy duds, too."

He tried not to groan at the sweet suction of her lips. "The first dance."

"The cake." She put the bag aside.

Which was good, since he didn't think he could bear seeing her licking anything again without letting the sensual maneuver spur him into action, too. He cleared his throat. "The honeymoon."

She sighed more wistfully than ever, then met his gaze. "It's too late for all that now."

"Is it?" Clint challenged her, hating to see her fall short of any of her fantasies when it wasn't necessary.

"What are you saying?"

He pulled her onto his lap and cuddled her close. "That you're still young. You have your whole life ahead of you. There's no reason to curtail your dreams."

She laid her head on his shoulder. Sighed again, looking upward. "There are three of them sleeping above us."

He stroked a hand lovingly through her hair. "Three who would like nothing better than to see their mommy happy."

He kissed the nape of her neck, her cheek, the shell of her ear.

Her phone rang.

Rose groaned and started to push away. "See what I mean? It's always something."

He tightened his arms around her. "Don't answer it."

She let it go. He kissed her—for real this time. The phone kept on ringing. She groaned again, and this time she did reach for it. Sprawled half on and half off his lap, she listened, her frown deepening.

"Of course I can be there. Yes, I'll get the message to him. Thanks." She hung up, looking stunned.

Concerned, he asked, "What's going on?"

Rose shook her head as if to clear it. "That was Jeff. He said they're delaying any additional filming."

Clint tensed. "Until when?"

"He didn't say. He did say he and the ad team and Farmtech execs all want to have lunch with both of us tomorrow at the Wagon Wheel restaurant in town."

Clint watched the quick rise and fall of her chest and wondered if he had gone too far. "You think they're firing me?"

Rose relaxed ever so slightly. She settled back on his lap, her mood pensive now. "Unlikely. I mean—" she raked her teeth across her lower lip "—if they wanted to do that, they could just do it via phone or email. There'd be no reason to invite us both to lunch."

"Maybe it will turn out to be good news." At least, Clint hoped—for Rose's sake—that was the case.

Chapter Thirteen

"Sorry we're late," Jeff said Friday at noon as he and Clint breezed into the party room at the Wagon Wheel restaurant, where everyone else was already gathered. "We were finalizing a deal for Clint's new tractor."

Ted perked up. "Which one is he purchasing?" he asked the local dealership owner.

Jeff grinned. "The TW466."

Or in other words, Rose thought, having looked at a few tractors herself, the very top of the line. "Congratulations." She smiled. Maybe they'd make a farmer out of Clint after all. Especially since a lot of ranchers also grew their own hay and feed for their herds.

Clint slipped into a chair next to Rose. Jeff took the one between Aaron and Ted.

To her relief, Clint not only looked the part of a businessman, in a sport coat, shirt, tie and jeans but also was behaving with more professional savvy.

During the meal, the conversation stayed casual, and they all got to know each other a little better. Finally, when the plates had been cleared and coffee and dessert served, it was time to get down to brass tacks. "I'm sure you're wondering why we asked you both here today," Ted began.

Rose had been afraid Clint was going to get fired.

Clearly, though, that wasn't the case, given the jocularity of everyone involved.

"We want to hire Rose to work on the campaign, too," Ted said. "At the same hourly rate we're already paying Clint."

Rose could only stare. "Excuse me?"

Aaron sipped his coffee. "You and Clint may both be too young to remember, but years ago, there was an iconic ad campaign for an instant camera that advertising professionals still look to for inspiration. The two spokespeople had such great chemistry that the public was convinced they were married in real life. And they were—but to other people." He paused for a moment. "Anyway, we have seen that same fun and sexy rapport in the two of you. And we all agree that *together* the two of you have the perfect combination of star power, sex appeal and knowledge."

Aaron brought out a stack of photos taken during the shooting. Not the stiff formal ones they had tried to take of Clint, but candid ones of Clint and Rose talking, flirting, laughing and arguing. Ones in which they both were silent, gazing deep into each other's eyes. In another, she was touching his arm, encouraging him, and he was staring down at her as if he were about to say to hell with everything, haul her into his arms and kiss her. *Really* kiss her.

"You have that rare ability to communicate without words." Aaron hit a button and handed over a computer tablet.

On screen was the footage of Rose talking enthusiastically about the berry picker and fruit harvesting. Her face was all lit up. Clint was standing nearby, grinning and listening intently.

"See?" Ted said, as if all their problems had been solved. "It's magic."

It was. And yet…

Rose struggled against the guilt. "I don't want to take any work from Clint," she said.

Or feel she was pushing him out of the limelight, because that would not be good for their relationship. And they did have a relationship, she realized, much as she kept trying to deny it.

Those photos, the film of them together, proved it.

Beside her, Clint was deep in thought, too. Finally he squinted at the execs, rocked back in his chair and asked, "Are you sure you don't want just Rose?"

He wanted her to go it alone?

Rose regarded Clint in shock.

He lifted a staying hand. "When it comes to farming and harvesting, and crops in Texas, she's really the expert."

Ted smiled in response. "Rose is great, and she does have the McCabe family name and reputation, which is always a plus, of course. But she's not a rodeo star turned Texas rancher. Bottom line, we need you both." In a smooth, businesslike tone, he elaborated, "Clint, your daily pay will stay the same. There will just be more of it than we originally envisioned, which will be covered in an addendum to your current agreement with Farmtech." Ted pushed a piece of paper at Rose. "This is what you can expect to earn."

Rose glanced at the paper. The sum was enough to put her in the black for the year!

Determined not to make the same mistake they'd made before, however, she played it cool. "Obviously I need to think about this for a day or two and talk to Clint. Make sure we're of the same mind. And my attorney will need to review any contracts."

"And any change to mine," Clint added.

Ted sobered. "We need an answer by tomorrow."

Rose and Clint exchanged looks, partners now in more ways than one. "No problem," they said in unison.

CLINT WALKED ROSE OUT, aware the luncheon couldn't have gone better, at least from his point of view. She looked incredibly pretty in a fitted white business suit and heels he guessed were from her pharmaceutical-rep days back in Dallas.

"So when and where do you want to talk?" Clint murmured when they reached the parking lot. The day was warm, and he took off his sport coat.

Rose glanced at her watch. "I have two and a half hours before I have to pick up the kids, but I need to go to Rose Hill Farm and do a few things first." She paused. "Can you follow me there in your pickup?"

He nodded, glad they'd have time alone without interruption, even if it was brief. "No problem," he said, already loosening his tie.

Fifteen minutes later, they were getting out of their vehicles and walking onto her front porch. The moment she opened her door, they were hit with the most delicious aroma. Aware he could get used to this, Clint mugged for her pleasure, "Mmm. Something sure smells fantastic."

She laughed. "It's blackberry jam. I've been cooking it in my Crock-Pot. I've got to get it into the mason jars I sterilized in the dishwasher this morning. You can help if you want."

"Sure."

Actually, there were three Crock-Pots around the kitchen, all filled with thick, bubbling jam. Following his lead and deciding to get more comfortable, too, Rose took off her jacket, revealing a pale blue satin tank top. She whipped on one of her flowery aprons with a bib across the chest. The sight of her was so sweet and homey, he got hard even before they stood together, shoulders bumping, washing their hands at the kitchen sink.

Figuring there was only one panacea for that, Clint caught her reaching for a towel and took her in his arms.

"Before we get started…" He lowered his head and kissed her the way he had wanted to all day, one hand running down her spine to rest at the small of her back. She curled against him like a heat-seeking kitten. Yet he was the one practically purring when the sensual liplock came to a halt.

She gazed up at him as if she would never really understand him. "What was that for?" she asked, dreamy-eyed.

A down payment for later, he thought. *A down payment for the rest of our lives.* But aware it was too soon for that, he said huskily instead, "Congratulations."

She laughed, her confusion deepening. "For stealing your job? Or half of it, anyway?"

Guilt ran through him at the machinations he'd used to help make that all happen. "I'm happy for you, Rose," he told her. And he was—although he would have preferred to be done with working for Farmtech, for good.

It just wasn't his thing.

The question was, how would he get out of it?

Without her losing out, too?

Rose moved away from him. She turned on the burner under two big canning tubs that had already been filled with water. While the water heated, she pulled out the sterilized mason jars. Handing him a ladle, she demonstrated how to fill each of the jars to within a quarter inch of the top with the hot jam. Once they began to work, she said, "I'm happy, too. I mean, according to the specifics they gave us over lunch, it's not going to require all that much time from either of us once we get the initial commercials and videos done. Just one or two days a month and a little bit of travel."

She paused to show him how to put the seals and lids on the filled jars.

"And best of all," she continued as she went down the line, wiping down the outside of the jars, "the money I'll get from Farmtech will pay all three of my kids' preschool tuition for an entire year!"

Together they carefully lowered the jars into the boiling water bath. Rose set the timer for ten minutes. She returned to the counter, then, with his help, carried the empty Crock-Pot insets to the farmhouse sink. "I mean, once they get to public school in another two years, the tuition won't be such an issue," she said, filling them all with hot, soapy water, then leaving them to soak. "But right now, I have to admit, it's pretty steep..."

As was her workload, Clint thought.

He was used to working hard himself, but as always, seeing her stretched to the limit filled him with need. And not just to hold her in his arms and make love to her. He wanted to protect and care for her, and her kids. Have fun with her. Weather the storms with her. He wanted... Hell, he wanted all of this. Just not with Farmtech.

She turned toward him again, stopped. The buzzer went off on the stove. She gave him another long, considering look.

He shook off his musing. "What do you need?"

She pointed to the stove. "All of these jars have to come out of the water and be set onto the towels on the counter to cool."

"I can do that." He stepped in to grab the handles and lift one of the wire racks that held the jars. He set it down gently. Then he turned to the second.

When he'd finished, Rose turned off the stove. She swung back to him. Her eyes were solemn, assessing, and in that split second, so very, very sad. "You really don't want to do this, do you?"

What was Clint supposed to say to that? He could lie, of course, but she would see right through him. "I think you're perfect for the position," he said finally.

She slipped off her apron. In the tank top and suit skirt,

she looked incredibly beautiful and feminine. Like the woman she had been before kids. The woman she still could be.

If he cooperated.

She sent him a skeptical look from beneath her lashes. "But you're not?"

He took his tie off and unfastened another button on his shirt. "I think I've made it clear advertising is really not my thing."

Her gaze focused on the open collar of his shirt. "So, if we were being completely honest with each other…" Dragging in a breath, she lifted her eyes to his once again. "You wouldn't want to do it at all. You'd want to finish what you were already under contract for and be done with it."

She understood him all too well.

But this wasn't just about him.

It was about her, too.

And what she'd negotiated for them both thus far had just enabled him to pay a sizable down payment on the top-of-the-line multipurpose tractor that would turn his property back into the horse and cattle ranch it was meant to be.

So if he had to sacrifice some of what he wanted in the short run, so be it. "Of course I want to spend time with you," he said honestly. "I want you to have a chance to promote your business and your expertise, too. Not to mention benefit financially."

He knew how much she struggled as a single mom, so he'd do anything that he could to make her life easier. And as a consequence, give the two of them more time to spend together—so he could convince her that what they had was a lot more than a fling.

"You're sure?"

Aware she still sensed something was off, he said, "Very."

Clint took her in his arms. Meaning, at that moment, to

simply distract. To keep her from asking any more point-blank questions that would force him either to lie or to tell the truth and hurt her feelings. Neither option was palatable. Making love to her—and cementing how far they'd come—was.

ROSE BARELY HAD time to react before Clint's head lowered. His eyes darkened. His lips fastened over hers. And just that suddenly, all her worries fled—along with the sinking sensation she had been in this exact same situation before. When she'd been with a man who was telling her everything was fine, though deep down, her feminine intuition knew otherwise.

It was obvious that whatever reservations Clint had possessed were gone as well, replaced by the here and now of this riveting kiss. She moaned softly as he clasped her to him and deepened the kiss until it was so wild and reckless she lost her breath. Unable to turn away from such pure unleashed need, such undeniable tenderness, she went up on tiptoe and pressed her breasts against the hardness of his chest, her lower half against his.

This, she thought, was the way she had always wanted to be kissed but never had been. As if he meant to erase every bit of hurt or disappointment she had ever weathered. Passion swept through her, and she kissed him back without restraint, letting everything she felt, everything she hoped for, pour into the smoldering embrace.

Clint rocked against her. "Rose," he rasped once, and then again. He captured her mouth and kissed her in a way that had her senses spinning and her heart soaring. "I want to make love to you…"

She'd been thinking they didn't have time, but the possessive glint in his eyes robbed her of the will to resist.

"Then we'd better hurry," she teased, glancing over their shoulder at the kitchen clock. "Because we've got exactly…thirty minutes…"

Tucking an arm beneath her knees, he carried her up the stairs and down the hall to her bedroom. "Plenty of time," he drawled, mischief lifting the corners of his mouth.

Her heart raced as he set her down beside the bed.

Not one to delay, he had her undressed in no time flat. She managed the same. The wicked gleam in his eyes igniting all her erogenous zones, he joined her on the bed. He rolled to face her, and she could feel him, hard and ready. And then his lips were on hers in a frenzy of wanting. She trembled as he cupped her breasts, caressing the taut, aching tips. Caressed the flatness of her abdomen, the sensitive inside of her thighs, and yes, there, too. The mind-blowing intimacy of his touch, coupled with his hot, knowing kisses, had her arching against him, taking in what he gave, soaking in the heat and sturdy masculine feel of him.

On the brink, she rolled him onto his back and moved on top of him. Draping her body over his, she caught his head between her hands and took the lead, kissing him languidly at first, then with building ardor, rubbing against him, driving him to the brink, even as the ridge of his arousal grew ever harder.

Liking the fact he was willing to let her set the pace, she slid ever lower, kissing and caressing, not stopping until he was throbbing every bit as much as she was.

And then they were changing places again; he was kissing her intimately, too, parting her thighs with his knee and rising above her. She gasped as he surged into her slick, wet heat. Wanting. Needing. Giving. Taking. As lovers, as equals, as friends.

He took everything she offered. She possessed him as well. Until there was nothing but the heart and soul of the moment, nothing but the two of them, and the never-ending, all-encompassing bliss.

Afterward they clung together. He captured her lips

in another hot, lingering kiss. "That was…amazing," he murmured finally.

Rose smiled at the wonder in his voice. Eyes closed, she laid her head on his chest and took in the steady beat of his heart. "It was," she murmured back. She liked the sexy turn their relationship had taken as much as the rough sound of his voice.

So what if he hadn't said he loved her? She hadn't said she loved him yet, either. Even though she was beginning to feel like she did.

Aware of the time crunch, they got up and began to dress. He watched her shimmy into her undies with undisguised pleasure. "You look…happy."

So did he.

Wishing they had time to make love again, Rose smiled as she went to the closet to get a pair of shorts and another knit top to put on in lieu of her business suit.

"I am happy, and excited, and thrilled about the idea of working with you and sometimes traveling with you for the entire next year." She nestled against him briefly before going to get a brush for her hair. "I guess I didn't realize it, but maybe even with all my business success and the joy I get from bringing up my kids, my life has been in a rut in other ways."

"Romantic ways?"

She nodded, admitting, "I'm finally ready for something more."

He took her in his arms and kissed her again. "That's good to hear."

Miraculously, Rose thought, the two of them were on the same page. Would wonders never cease?

"THANKS FOR MEETING me on such short notice," Clint told Amy Carrigan-McCabe later that same afternoon when she arrived at the Double Creek.

"How can I help you?" the energetic blonde asked, getting out of her Laurel Valley Ranch pickup truck, clipboard in hand.

Knowing the plant nursery owner was also one of the best botanists in the area, Clint strode forward to shake her hand. "I wanted to talk to you about possibly moving the blackberry bushes on my property. Is there any way to dig up and transplant them?"

"Not with any real hope of success."

"Is there another way to grow more of them, then?"

Amy pushed her sunglasses up on top of her head. "We can propagate them from leafy stem cuttings and root cuttings."

Clint wanted to be sure he understood. "So the very same bushes I have on my property now—"

"Can be duplicated elsewhere. Basically, there are two ways to do it," she explained. "The most economical way is to take leafy stem cuttings when the canes are still actively growing and place the cuttings in a moist mix of peat and sand until the roots begin to grow."

That did sound easy enough.

"With root cuttings, we wait until the plants are dormant— which is sometime in the fall or winter, depending on the weather—to take the root cuttings. Those go into cold storage for three weeks and then are planted in a peat and soil mixture, covered in clear plastic, and set in a warm place until roots appear. In either case, once we get good, healthy roots established, we can plant the new bushes in gardens or fields."

He nodded, stroking his jaw with one hand. "And how long before they would produce the kind of yield I've got now?"

She looked at his fields. "I'd say at least five years."

Not good. Trying not to think how this news would devastate Rose, Clint pushed on. "Okay, here's my next question. You're familiar with Rose's property. Is there a place blackberries could be planted at Rose Hill Farm with good results?"

Amy's face lit up. "Oh, absolutely."

"Are there other places in Laramie County that would be equally hospitable?"

"Yes. A lot, actually." Amy paused. "I'm not sure what you're trying to do here, Clint."

Make Rose happy.

Make myself happy.

Make everyone happy.

Clint shrugged, then finally said, "I don't want my ranch to be the only place these blackberries can be found."

Amy rocked back on the heels of her boots. "That's mighty generous of you."

Not really, given what he'd also be mowing down in the process. That was going to make more than a few people upset. Especially Rose. Which was why he had to do damage control now. Clint shoved a hand through his hair. "I was thinking about giving some Double Creek blackberry bushes to Rose, since she's become so fond of them."

Amy smiled. "That's really nice. Very…sentimental."

He nodded, sure hoping that Rose would see it that way, too. "So, you'll work up an action plan and cost estimate for me?" he pressed. "I want to make sure that Rose knows what would be involved and approves the plan before we proceed."

"Sure. No problem."

"Great," he said with a big sigh of relief. "I'd also like a list of any other local farmers or landowners you think might be interested in growing Double Creek blackberries, too—so I can talk to them about it when the time comes. Naturally, I'd hire your business to do the work, which is why I asked you out here."

"All sounds good to me." Amy tossed her clipboard into the seat of her pickup truck. "It's going to take a few days for me to work up the proposal, though."

"That's fine. In the meantime, I'd appreciate it if you didn't mention this to Rose or anyone else. It's kind of hard to explain...but I'd like it to be a surprise for her when I do tell her."

Amy mimed a zipper across her mouth. "I understand. My lips are sealed."

Unfortunately, just as Amy drove off, Rose and her kids arrived at the ranch. Rose got out of the driver's seat while Clint assisted the kids. Then Scarlet, Stephen and Sophia ran up to the front porch to get the Matchbox car set Clint had brought out for them.

Grinning, Rose ambled toward him. "Did Amy finally come out to talk to you about getting some plants?"

He nodded.

Assuming—wrongly—that her cousin's wife had initiated the conversation, Rose continued cheerfully, "Well, I'd take her up on it if I were you. Could be a lot of money for you there." She winked. "Not to mention what sharing the plants would do for the community at large."

Reluctant to let anything spoil the evening ahead, Clint passed on the opportunity to correct Rose's misconception. Instead, he gathered her against him for a welcoming hug. "Hey," he chided gently, "I thought you were all here for pony rides and a picnic supper!"

"We are," the kids shouted from the porch.

He pointed to the corral next to the barn, where the Shetland Pony he had borrowed for the occasion waited. "Then let's get to it."

"More hugs, Mr. Clint. More hugs!" the triplets said as they were leaving.

Aware it was several hours past their bedtime and

they were all blissfully tired, Rose looked at her children. "Okay. But this is the last round. You-all have a big day tomorrow. Speaking of which…"

She paused and turned to Clint. This was a big step. She was ready for it.

He looked at her, waiting.

Rose bolstered her courage. "There's a family barbecue being hosted by my Aunt Annie and Uncle Travis. It's at their ranch—the Triple Diamond. I'm allowed to bring a date." She swallowed around her sudden burst of nerves, aware she hadn't put her heart on the line this way in quite a while, if ever. "So, if you're interested…?"

Without warning, he played hard to get. "Depends."

She caught the mischief in his eyes and returned it in kind. "Really. On what?"

He tapped a finger against his chin, thinking. "Are you going to wear a dress or jeans?"

Rose tried not to think what fun he'd had getting her out of a dress. "Most likely capris," she said, trying not to blush at the sensual memories. "Why? Does that make a difference?"

Very aware—as was she—that the kids were listening to every word, he said, "I was thinking we should *match*. Like," he gestured dramatically, "if you wore jeans, I'd wear jeans. Or, if you wore a dress…" he hesitated long enough to make her heart race "…I'd wear chinos and a button-down. But—" he paused dramatically yet again, while the kids and Rose all hung on his every word "—I don't have any capris."

Rose rolled her eyes.

The kids giggled.

Solemnly she told him, "I'd be worried if you did have capris." Wishing she could pull him into her arms and kiss him senseless right then and there, she patted him on the cheek and declared, "But no worries, cowboy. Jeans and a shirt are fine."

He sighed as if greatly relieved.

The kids giggled again.

Rose had to hide a smile.

Until her next thought hit. "Speaking of button-downs. Do you still have that shirt my kids ruined?"

He sobered, too. "Yeah. Why?"

"Well, I'd like to see if I can't work my magic and have it looking like new again."

He frowned. "You don't have to do that."

Yeah, she did. The guilt had been weighing on her. "It's either that or buy you a new one in the exact same size, style and color," she told him archly. "Which, by the way, I'm thinking about doing anyway."

He held up a hand. "Don't do that. I'll get the shirt for you."

"Thank you."

He was only gone a couple of minutes, but by the time he returned, she'd managed to get the children securely buckled up inside her SUV. And a typically nonsensical preschool discussion was already underway.

"Mommy, how come you didn't get to ride the pony and we all did?" Sophia asked.

"Yeah, it's not fair!" Stephen chimed in. "Why couldn't you?"

"Because I am too big. Isn't that right, Mr. Clint?" She gave him a pointed look from the driver's seat when he handed over the shirt.

"Absolutely," he replied. A smile tugged at the corner of his lips as he opened the rear passenger door and leaned in. Their booster seats were lined up across the middle bench. "Ponies are for little children. Horses are for big kids and adults. And as it happens, I have gone riding with your mom earlier this week. So…it is fair. Everyone has had a pony or horsey ride, okay?"

Silence fell as they all ruminated on that.

"Can we do it again?" Scarlet finally asked.

"We sure can," Clint promised.

Which was, Rose thought wistfully, a very nice idea.

He quirked a brow at the kids. "You-all ready to go home now?"

"Nooooo!" the triplets shouted in unison.

"Well, you have to be because I am about to dole out the final hugs goodbye. Okay, here goes," he teased. "One hug for you, one for you, and one for you! And because she's been such a good sport all day, a—"

Rose braced herself for him to come around to her side and plant a big kiss against her cheek.

"— simple wave for Mommy!" Clint stepped back to comically bid her adieu.

She narrowed her eyes at him. The triplets all dissolved into laugher, as they were meant to.

"I owe you one," she mouthed at him as she started the engine, wondering all the while what she had ever done without him.

He leaned in and gave her a G-rated hug anyway. "And you can bet I will be there to collect."

Rose was counting on it.

VIOLET CAME OVER the next morning to help Rose make cobblers for the family barbecue.

"You're doing Clint's laundry now?"

Rose knew that was a couple thing, but not in this case. Here, it was mainly guilt and responsibility at play. She held the blue-and-white tattersall up to the light. "Just the one the kids messed up." Which now also happened to be Clint's lucky shirt.

Violet eyed the stain. "Have you already pretreated it?"

Rose nodded. "A couple of times. I think the mustard and ketchup sat too long on the fabric. Either that—" she went to work with another concoction of dish soap, white vinegar and water and began to see some improvement "—or the stains really set while they were in the dryer, after they were washed the first time."

Violet lifted her brow. "I hate to say it, but I think it might be a hopeless cause."

Giving up on this would be like giving up on…well, her and Clint. "There has to be a way." Rose went back to the washer and set it on the soak cycle.

"Why is it so important to you when you could easily go out and buy a replacement?"

Exactly what Clint had said.

"You're not trying to show Clint how good a wife you could be to him, are you?"

"Come on, Violet. You know how I feel about marriage." Rose had crashed and burned at it once. She wasn't about to do it again.

"I know how you used to feel. But in the past few weeks, something's changed."

Violet was right. Something *had* changed.

And Rose was still thinking about that when Clint arrived to pick her and the kids up.

As they loaded the desserts and the kids into the back of her SUV, she couldn't help but think about how quickly she and Clint and the kids had come to feel like family.

She loved being with him like this. The kids adored their group adventures, too.

Maybe it was time she rethought her stance on her own happily-ever-after.

And, as it happened, Rose wasn't the only one who was pleased Clint was around.

"I'm so glad you came today and brought Clint," her Aunt Annie said shortly after they arrived. "I'm working on a new line of fresh fruit–based barbecue sauce and marinades, and I'd really like to use Double Creek blackberries. Do you think Clint would be interested in setting some aside for my company?"

Rose smiled. "We can ask."

Together they went to talk to Clint.

Although he readily agreed to provide Annie McCabe with any of the produce that was not already spoken for, he was not as thrilled as Rose had expected him to be.

"Is everything okay?" she asked after they had strolled away. Being a supplier for Annie's Homemade was a major coup!

Clint waved at the triplets, who were busy playing tag with their cousins, then went to her SUV to bring in the cobblers. "I didn't know this was going to be a business meeting."

"It wasn't." Rose carried one, too. "That was just a conversation." But she knew he had a point. Today was supposed to be their only day off all week, the event a fun-filled party. Still…this was a McCabe gathering, and a lot of their family businesses were linked in some way.

"People always talk shop at social gatherings," she added as they walked onto the screened-in back porch and set the dishes on the buffets already set up.

He grimaced. "Not always, Rose."

Rose sized up the tense set of his broad shoulders. "You're really going to stay mad at me over this?"

He shook his head. "Not mad. Frustrated."

Was this their first fight—as a couple? She only knew she did not want it to be. Not on a beautiful day like today. Not when their relationship—and it *was* a relationship— was going so well.

She'd had one failed union.

She was not about to have another.

Rose glanced around. Seeing the kids were still well-supervised, she took Clint's wrist in hand. "Well, then," she told him defiantly, "you leave me no choice."

She skirted the house, then led him beyond an impossibly long row of SUV's and pickup trucks. "Now what are you doing?" he asked wryly.

Rose dragged him behind the barn, aware she hadn't felt this brazen in, well, forever.

She wound her arms about his neck and went up on tiptoe. "I'm collecting on that kiss you owe me—from last night."

He put his hands on her shoulders, his expression stern. "Someone could come by."

"No," Rose said just as stubbornly, "they won't. And even if they did," she rushed on impulsively, "I don't care." She pressed her lips to his, wanting him to know that it wasn't just business bringing them together. It wasn't just sex or friendship or the way he was with her kids. It was so much more than that. She felt it every time they were together, and she could tell by the way he was kissing her back, first sweetly and tenderly, and then hotly and without restraint, that he felt it, too. And that was when they heard the distinct cough.

The kind meant to interrupt.

Rose and Clint broke apart abruptly. Pivoted around and then saw, to Rose's dismay, none other than her father, Jackson McCabe.

"IT'S NOT A BIG DEAL," Rose said moments later, after her father had departed.

"Really?" Clint grumbled, thinking it a very big deal that the parent of a woman he was serious about had just gotten the idea that he was anything but honorable. This wasn't how he wanted to start a dialogue with Rose's dad. And it certainly wasn't how he had been brought up. "Because I think if we hadn't already been *behind* the barn, your dad would have taken us both there."

Rose rolled her eyes. "He barely said anything."

Clint caught her hand in his, furious with himself, because instead of protecting her as was his intent, he had made her vulnerable. Although Rose did not seem to realize that. "One disapproving lift of the eyebrow was enough, don't you think?"

Rose walked toward a pasture, where some of the ranch horses were grazing. She leaned against the railing, looking out at the pastoral scene. "It was just a knee-jerk reaction. The kind he always had when we were teens."

Aware this was the kind of setup he wanted for himself— with cattle and horses on different parts of the land—Clint took a place next to Rose. "So you and your sisters made a habit of this?"

"No," she said, chagrined. "I was the one who always seemed to get caught kissing my boyfriend."

Clint's jaw tightened. He didn't want to think about Rose in the arms of anyone else. "I gather it hasn't happened lately?" he asked, studying the hint of sun-blushed color across her cheeks. "Not even with those three guys you dated recently?"

"Nope." She shook her head. "Not in maybe…ten… years." She gazed at him from beneath her lashes. "What about you, cowboy?"

Figuring she already knew the answer to that, he smirked. "I haven't acted like a love-struck teenager in about that amount of time, either."

"Teenager, huh?" She seemed pleased.

"What can I say?" He shrugged, took her hand in his and looked deep into her eyes. "I've got a thing for you."

Her expression softened in the way he loved so much. "And I have a thing for you," she whispered.

Silence fell between them, easy now.

Figuring it was his turn to risk something, too, he took her all the way in his arms, lowered his head and kissed her with all his heart.

Chapter Fourteen

"Do you mind leaving for Dallas a little early?" Rose asked Clint the following week after they had unloaded the blackberries. "Say, Thursday noon instead of evening?"

Farmtech had offered to put them up in a downtown Dallas hotel so they'd be rested and refreshed for the meetings and contract signings scheduled for Friday morning and the introduction to select members of the agricultural press, set for later in the day.

"Sounds good to me." He came closer, his low voice heightening her anticipation of their trip and rare time alone even more. He threaded a hand through her hair, his gaze skimming her upturned face. "Any particular reason why?"

In no hurry—since her kids were on an after-school play date that included dinner—Rose leaned against the closed barn doors. "A very good one, as a matter of fact. Fresh Foods Market in Dallas heard about the blackberries. They've asked me to bring in a truckload for their metroplex stores."

Clint nodded, understanding what a boon that would be for both their businesses, even as he asked, "Will there be enough?"

Rose nodded, explaining, "It'll be the last big harvest.

After that, I think the yield will be a lot smaller, and then disappear entirely within a week. At least until next year."

She tried not to feel too sad about that or think about what that would mean in terms of daily visits from Clint. After all, they didn't need an outside reason to see each other.

And she wanted to keep seeing him, she realized. She wanted him to be a permanent fixture in her and her kids' lives.

She moved away from him, still struggling with the knowledge of just how deep her affection for him was, of how very much she wanted them to have a future together.

Trying not to worry whether or not he was just as serious about her and the kids, she swallowed. "Anyway, we can get them all picked and crated by late Wednesday and keep the fruit refrigerated in the barn overnight. I'll get co-op members to help load up the truck again on Thursday morning, and we can take off after that."

He waited while she cut him a check for the previous week's crop. "I assume we're taking two vehicles?"

Realizing how amazing he looked, even with his hair all windblown and a day's shadow of beard lining his handsome face, she nodded. "We can park my SUV at the hotel, but not the refrigerated truck. The store said I can leave that at their distribution center until I leave Friday night." So at least she didn't have to worry about finding a place to park it in the city.

Clint caught her wrist, lifted it over her head, and spun her around in an unexpected dance move that ended with her dipped back over his arm. "Do we have time for a date Thursday evening?"

Heart pounding, she wreathed her arms about his shoulders and batted her eyelashes flirtatiously. "Are you asking me out?"

He leaned closer and brushed his lips against hers. "I

am. We have to work on that chemistry that so impressed the bigwigs."

Rose sighed wistfully and let him kiss her again, more thoroughly this time. "Then, yes," she breathed.

Slowly he brought her upright, slid his hands down her spine and cupped her against him. "Yes to the date?"

Her eyes sparkled. There was no mistaking his desire. Or hers. "Yes." She pressed her lips to his once, and then again. "To…everything."

To Rose's delight, all went smoothly on their trek to market. And it was even better once they arrived.

"The blackberries are every bit as good as everyone said they were," the regional produce manager from Fresh Foods Market said Thursday afternoon after sampling them. "How do you want us to advertise them? Under the Rose Hill Farm banner or the ranch where they originated?"

Wanting to give credit where it was due, Rose replied, "Let's go with Double Creek Ranch blackberries since that's where they originated."

"Are you sure you don't want to sell them under the Rose Hill Farm name?" Clint asked. He shrugged his broad shoulders amiably. "Your business is more widely known for all sorts of quality local produce."

And hence had better name recognition.

But they were from his land! Didn't he feel the pride in that? The emotional connection to such a great crop? Shouldn't he want the credit?

"Clint has a point," the produce manager interjected. "It might mean more to the consumer."

Clint nodded. "Better sales benefit us all."

"Okay. You fellas have convinced me." Pushing aside any residual guilt she felt at stealing the thunder from his ranch, Rose smiled and accepted a check. They all shook hands. Then she and Clint headed for the hotel.

Once there, Rose wasn't surprised to find their rooms were located on the concierge level. Farmtech had promised to give them luxury accommodations. Nonetheless, she was stunned to realize their rooms opened onto a shared living room and a balcony with a breathtaking city view.

With no kids to care for and the rest of the afternoon and evening stretching out ahead of them, the situation was suddenly filled with endless romantic possibilities. "Our dinner reservations aren't until eight," Clint said, gathering her in his arms. He gave her a squeeze and bussed her temple. "So we have plenty of time if you want to lie down."

Actually, she did.

He caught her mischievous grin.

"I was thinking, rest."

Rose wasn't. She turned, gliding her hands across the solid warmth of his chest. "Are you tired?"

Eyes crinkling at the corners, he cupped her face in his large hands. "No."

"Neither am I." She reached up and gave him a light, lingering kiss that was both a celebration of the moment and a down payment for later. Reluctantly she broke off the embrace. "I do feel a little grungy, though." She closed her eyes with a little moan, luxuriating in the feeling of his fingers entwined in her hair. "Want to check out the showers?"

He chuckled with undisguised affection, then let her go long enough to slip his arm around her waist. "Good idea."

They walked into her bedroom. A king-size bed outfitted with sumptuous white hotel linens and a half dozen pillows dominated the plushly carpeted room. Beyond a luxurious dressing room was another door. They moved past it, into a large marble bathroom with a glassed-in shower and a sunken tub big enough for two. There were plenty of thick, fluffy towels, two spa robes, and an array of scented soaps, lotions and bubble baths.

Rose drew a deep breath, imagining the pleasure that could be had. Impulsively she turned to face him. "Care to join me?"

"What do you think?"

Rose knew what she hoped. That this evening would be their most sexy and romantic yet!

Clint grinned as if reading her mind. He caught her against him for another tantalizing kiss that had her heart racing. Then he drew back, his eyes dark and intent. "I'll be back in ten minutes." He gave her another brief, affectionate squeeze then disappeared.

Rose started the water and put in a generous amount of the fragrant bubble bath. She went back to turn down her bed, then returned to the bath. Quickly she washed the grime off her face, brushed her teeth and swept her hair into an updo off her neck. She had just stripped down and slid into the chest-high bubbles when a knock sounded on the door.

Clint strolled in with his usual innate grace. He dispensed with his robe and set it aside in a way that left her mouth dry.

Like her, he was already physically, visibly aroused. *Oh. My.* She flashed her best come-hither smile. "Come on in. The water's fine."

He tipped an imaginary hat, seeming to like what he saw as much as she did. "Don't mind if I do."

She was trembling as he settled opposite her. The tub was just big enough for him to stretch out his legs on either side of her. She took the back of his hand and kissed the inside of his wrist, loving the warm, masculine texture of his skin. Unable to help herself, she teased, "Is this how you imagined our evening beginning?"

Clint released a gusty sigh, then took her fingertips and sucked the ends of them gently, one by one. "Ah. No." He reached out and touched her cheek. "I thought I was going to have to woo you."

She shivered in response, aware this was all turning very sensual very fast. A fact that made her very, very happy. She gazed into his eyes, loving the fact they were alone again and doing something deliciously sexy…and forbidden. "And here it's all so easy."

His gaze grew serious, intent. "Some things are just meant to be," he said huskily. Catching her wrist, he tugged her forward until she settled between his legs, her thighs wrapped around his waist, her arms on his shoulders. "This better?"

Making love with Clint was so much better than she ever could have imagined it would be. Rose pressed her breasts against his chest and rubbed lightly. "We're getting there."

"How about this?" His hands slid down her hips, and he fit her against him, softness to hardness, woman to man. He trailed his lips over her ear, her neck, then her lips.

They kissed wantonly, deeply.

"And this." Aware being so close to him felt so right, Rose lathered soap between her hands and spread the fragrant bubbles over his chest, down his back, down the length of his arms. He shifted, giving her access to his thighs. Then, between subsequent kisses, slowly and lovingly, he did the same for her.

Of course, what had been lathered up had to be rinsed. The sensitive places that had been denied the first go-round were found in the second, others in the third. And there were so many kisses, Rose noted euphorically, in between.

Finally Clint groaned and rested his forehead against hers. "Time we move this to the bedroom, don't you think?"

Good point. She was nearing completion now.

Rose chuckled. As their gazes met, the air between them reverberated with excitement and escalating desire. "Unless you know how to put a condom on under water..."

She watched his eyes darken as they roved over her jutting nipples and the curves of her breasts. She felt more womanly than she ever had in her life.

He stood lithely and, grasping her by the hand, brought her with him out onto the mat. Water and bubbles streamed down their bodies, the chill in the air an erotic counterpoint to the sizzling heat beneath their skin.

He caught her against him briefly, warming her with the length of his tall, powerful form, his arousal so pronounced, so smooth and velvety, she could hardly wait to have him inside her once again. Gallantly he wrapped her in a towel, then reached inside the pocket of his robe. Half a dozen condoms spilled out. "Can't say I've ever tried it in the tub," he admitted, gathering them up with one hand, taking her by the other. Naked and beautiful, he led her toward the bed and dried her off slowly and lovingly.

She lay down, watching as he took the towel and quickly dried himself off.

"Besides," he whispered, lying beside her and kissing her again, "I like you under me."

Rose watched as he opened the packet and swiftly, surely protected them both. She caught her breath at the passion still etched on his handsome face. "You do?"

"Mmm-hmm." Big hands intimately circling her hips, he shifted so she was astride him. "And on top."

She stretched out over him, kissing him sweetly, taking her time. His hand slid between them, stroking the tender insides of her thighs, finding the pleasure point, driving her crazy as more passionate kisses were exchanged. "Just so long," he said finally, lifting her and surging inside, "as you're in my arms."

And she was. Even as they took each other to new heights and lingered there, with the tenderness and need and singularity of purpose they both deserved.

Afterward, as they lay cuddled against each other, she knew this was what it felt like when it was right. This was what it felt like when love was about to happen. "Clint?" she murmured softly, her heart full, her body still humming deliciously.

He lifted his head, gazed into her eyes and simply waited.

Wrapping her arms around him, Rose snuggled even closer. She knew she was desperately close to making a complete and utter fool of herself, but she forced herself to bare her soul anyway. "I know what I said before. But I don't want this to be a temporary love affair." Her eyes filled with deep, searing emotion she identified as joy. "I want it to last."

Tightening his hold on her, Clint bent his head and kissed her again in a way that made her feel incredibly safe and cherished. "So do I, Rose." He brushed his lips reverently over hers. "So do I."

And then, she supposed, just so there would be no doubt, he made love to her all over again.

"Don't you two look like a couple of honeymooners," Aaron remarked the next day when Rose and Clint walked into their meeting with attorney Travis Anderson at their side.

Rose met Clint's eyes. He gave her an imperceptible look that reminded her of all they had shared the night before. A whisper of tenderness swept through her. She'd never had a more romantic, and satisfying, interlude in her life. Luckily for them, many more lay ahead.

"I guess that's why everyone thinks we're such great business partners," Rose replied with a mysterious smile.

"Because we're not just neighbors but good friends," Clint concurred.

"Well, whatever it is," the director of the advertising campaign noted with approval, "it clearly works."

With a murmur of agreement, everyone took a seat at the conference table, and the business meeting began.

"The clauses Rose asked for were approved and added," Ted announced. "Clint will receive the berry picker he's been using, free and clear, and the taxes on it will be paid by the corporation."

Gleefully Rose turned to Clint, who had a completely inscrutable expression on his face. "Surprise!" she said.

Ted grinned at her joke and continued, "Additionally, a steep lifetime discount has been arranged for any future Farmtech equipment that Rose and Clint wish to purchase for their prospective ranches. In return, the Farmtech legal department has added a few more clauses to the contract, too." Ted paused. "They're marked by the purple tabs in the copies we have printed out for review. So if everyone will take a look…"

Pages rustled.

The exec continued, "Basically, it says we reserve the right to send in a professional team to trim and mani-cure the blackberry fields at the Double Creek Ranch next spring, prior to and during the filming. And to make any visual or artistic adjustments necessary for filming."

Beside Rose, Clint stiffened, clearly displeased. "I thought we were done with that."

Rose had thought so, too. Especially since she knew how he had loathed having to stand around posing for the cameras.

Ted smiled. "For this year, yes, we are done with the on-location work at the Double Creek Ranch. But next year, we're also planning to send out teams of local news reporters and journalists to see a live and in-person demonstration of the berry picker."

His eyes narrowing, Clint told everyone, "But the fields won't be there."

Everyone stopped.

Gasping inaudibly, Rose felt herself freeze. She hadn't felt this blindsided since Barry had told her he didn't want kids, after all.

Yes, the clues had been there all along—then.

Had they been there this time, too?

She just hadn't wanted to notice them?

Given the hard, unyielding look on Clint's face, this was indeed the case.

Everyone looked at her as if to say, *Do something! Work your magic!* But how could she, when Clint clearly was of such a different mindset than everyone else in the room?

He continued, "I'm mowing down all hundred acres with the tractor I just bought. That's all going to be pastureland for my cattle and horses. So if you want to use footage of the Double Creek Ranch, that's fine with me, but it will have to be footage that's already been filmed this year."

A stunned silence fell.

"No one told me anything about this!" Ted said angrily. "We've designed a whole publicity campaign around that hundred-acre blackberry field! It was going to help us show how a former rodeo star turned successful farmer without losing an ounce of his sex appeal or lust for life in the process!"

Rose's heart sank. She had thought that to be the case, too.

But had it all been an illusion? Something she had needed and wanted to see for them to be a couple, but wasn't really there after all?

Rose did not have the answers to those questions.

However, she did know when a business arrangement she'd worked so hard to negotiate was about to implode.

Determined to salvage the deal before it went even further south, Rose stood, matter-of-factly made eye contact with everyone in the room, then said graciously, "I'm sorry for the confusion." She implied with a glance that it was all a simple mix-up that could be easily corrected. "Could I have a moment alone with Clint, please?"

She had been in stickier situations.

She could fix this, too.

With disgruntled sighs, everyone filtered out.

Finally she and Clint were alone in the elegantly appointed conference room. She walked over to where he now stood, at the windows overlooking downtown Dallas. "What are you doing?" To this deal? To himself? To *them*?

Hands shoved in the pockets of his trousers, he swung around to face her. "Exactly what I said I would do all along. Turning my family ranch back into a cattle and horse operation."

Maybe it was the fact that they were both in business clothes—a dark suit for him, a sheath and jacket for her—instead of their usual ranch attire, but suddenly he looked like a stranger to her. Worse, he seemed to be regarding her the same way.

Rose tipped her chin up. "You know the worth of the blackberry bushes. How unique and wonderful they are."

"I do. Which is why I asked Amy to come out and take a look and figure out what would be required to keep the line going."

Okay. That was *something*.

Handsome jaw set, Clint continued, "She's working up a proposal as we speak. To take root cuttings and plant some on your farm, and as many others as you like—or can arrange for—elsewhere, too."

Just not on his land.

Rose could not deny that her cousin's wife had not just an amazing plant nursery, but a way with growing and engineering plants that was unparalleled. "That's great, Clint, but it takes several years for new canes to produce a decent crop of blackberries."

His voice dropped persuasively. "But once they do, the plants can produce for fifteen to twenty years."

He was right. Long-range, his plan was fine, assuming they could duplicate the soil conditions at his place elsewhere.

He took her hand in his. "I know losing those fields is a temporary hit financially, Rose. For both of us. But there will be other monetary gain to be had by the sale of the root cuttings. And the work you're doing for Farmtech."

If that were all it was, it would be one thing. If she'd even seen this coming. But she hadn't. She'd thought the two of them were of the same mind and heart.

Only to find out she and Clint were as far apart in what they wanted as she and her ex.

She'd made a mistake that inadvertently involved her kids once. Was she about to make another?

Rose swallowed. She withdrew her hand from his and stepped back. Still feeling terribly betrayed, she pointed out, "Except there won't be any work for Farmtech for either of us if there's no berry patch at Double Creek."

"Sure there will. It may not be as the Farmtech team envisions it right now, but there will still be a berry picker to sell and a couple to sell it." His lips twisted in a rueful smile. "You heard them. We're like honeymooners. We have a chemistry that's at least unique and highly watchable, if not darn near iconic."

His joke citing the words of the ad execs fell flat.

She frowned at him, struggling not to cry. "Except that chemistry is a fake."

The rims of his eyes darkened. It was his turn to be

nonplussed, but she took no pleasure in that. "How do you figure that?" he asked gruffly.

Tension throbbed between them.

"Because if that chemistry were real, Clint, I wouldn't have to tell you how much those blackberries have come to mean to me." She spun away, unable to bear his nearness any longer. "I wouldn't have to explain to you how you are hurting and disappointing not just me but legions of other people. Our business colleagues. Our friends and neighbors. All our customers."

Nor would she be so shocked to find out the depth and breadth of the differences between them.

She balled her hands into fists at her sides. "You would know how much those berries mean to everyone who has enjoyed them this year. You would know it would be almost criminal to destroy them! Never mind give up the only reason you and I have to be together…"

Abruptly he looked as if he'd been the one blindsided with a punch to the gut. "Did you just say that those berries are the only reason we have to be together?"

She guessed she had. And for good reason. "That ad campaign for the harvester was going to have us working and traveling together all year long!" Bitterly she admitted to herself how much she had been looking forward to that, too.

He huffed in disgust. "So without it, we're over. Is that it?"

Were they?

Sadly, Rose realized that was indeed the case. Her shoulders hunched in defeat, she acknowledged, "I can't be involved with a man who doesn't want what I want again, Clint." It was just too miserable and ill-fated a situation. Because even if it didn't end now, it would surely end later.

A muscle worked in his jaw. "And I can't be involved with a woman who will be with me only if I meet her demands and adhere to whatever narrow definition of our life together that she has."

So their love affair was over.

Why was she not surprised? Maybe because all along she had known it was too good, too wonderful and special to be true.

Wearily she tried to salvage what they could. "Okay, fine. We won't be lovers anymore." They could keep a small part of what they had built, however, assuming she could figure out a way to salvage the deal with Farmtech. "We could still have a business partnership, Clint."

His gaze hardened. "No, Rose, we can't," he returned. "Not if we're not friends. And given the way we both feel, well, let's just say maybe we both should have seen this coming."

Giving her no chance to reply, Clint turned on his heel and walked out.

Chapter Fifteen

"Is that the contract?" Violet asked Saturday afternoon, shortly after closing, when she stopped by Rose Hill Farm to pick up a fresh supply of locally grown produce.

Putting the legal papers aside, Rose nodded and took the reusable mesh crate her triplet handed her.

Still in the scrubs she'd worn for her thirty-six-hour hospital shift, Violet followed Rose around the barn. "Did you get everything you wanted?"

Rose picked out several lush green zucchini and two equally delectable crookneck yellow squash from a colorful display. "From the Farmtech tractor company? Yes." It had taken ten days of nonstop negotiating between the execs and the lawyers and the "talent," but finally everyone was happy, and a new plan was in place.

Looking as peaked as usual after one of her long shifts, Violet added a head of cabbage and two large sweet onions to the stash. "So they agreed to let you be the sole spokesperson for the berry picker?"

Rose picked up another mesh basket for fruit and tried not to think about what a lonely prospect that was going to be. "Unless Clint changes his mind and decides to do it with me, and we both know that's unlikely." Sighing wearily, Rose pushed away the dreams of what might have been. "The truth is, he never wanted to do it in the first place." So the creative team behind the advertising had wisely decided to make do with what photo and film footage they had and let him out of the rest of his contract.

Violet added new red potatoes and a bunch of carrots to her basket. "Why do you think he agreed, then?"

"Because I pushed him into it," Rose said, guilt tightening her chest.

Violet made a dissenting face. She walked over to the cucumbers and selected a few. "Clint McCulloch doesn't strike me as the kind of man who gets steamrollered into anything he doesn't want to do, even if a pretty woman is doing the asking." She added a head of baby lettuce. "So why did he really say yes?"

Rose added strawberries, raspberries and blueberries to her basket, then paused in front of the new crop of yellow peaches. "To be perfectly honest, I don't have a clue why he ever agreed."

Regret lashed through her. It would have been so much simpler if he hadn't. They wouldn't have become friends. Or lovers. She wouldn't have fallen so hard and so fast for him. Wouldn't have wanted more… Violet carried her crate over to the cash register and set it down with a thud. She turned to Rose, hands on her hips. "Yeah, you do. You just don't want to say it."

Rose felt her breath hitch. Her sister was right. She didn't want to voice it because hearing it aloud made it real.

Irreversible.

Nor did she want to lament all she had lost.

And she had lost a tremendous amount, behaving as she had, insisting that he forget what he wanted for his ranch and do what she wanted for the Double Creek.

Her selfishness had gotten her in trouble before, when she'd wanted a baby despite her ex-husband's disinterest, and ended up raising triplets completely on her own.

She could have had a limited partnership with Clint.

Without any more Double Creek blackberries.

Instead she had stubbornly demanded it all.

And look where that had gotten her.

Utterly alone…and heartbroken.

Again.

Aware Violet was still waiting for an explanation, Rose sighed. "He agreed because he knew it would benefit us both financially." And at the end of the day, he was a businessperson, too. She had been counting on that fact from the very beginning.

Violet added a bunch of grapes to the fruit stash and carried it to the checkout counter. "Clint doesn't strike me as the kind of person who would do anything for money, either."

"Which is perhaps why the whole endeavor rubbed him the wrong way," Rose responded irritably. "Because he'd rather be true to himself and his own goals than toe someone else's line." *Like mine.*

Violet shrugged while Rose weighed and rang up the produce with mindless efficiency. "He looked pretty happy at the family barbecue. I heard the two of you were even caught making out behind the barn."

Rose stopped in her tracks. "Dad said something?" she asked, blushing furiously.

"To Mom," Violet confirmed with a nod. "Who in turn said something to me. She wanted to know how serious the two of you were."

Rose turned away from her sister's searching gaze. "Very, I thought at the time."

Violet paid what she owed. Together they carried her stash out to the car. "So what changed?"

It all would have seemed so foolish now, had it not been a concrete sign that she and Clint were all wrong for each other, and always would be. "He decided to mow down the hundred acres of prime blackberries on the Double Creek."

Violet lounged against her vehicle, arms folded in front of her. "Wasn't that his plan all along?"

Yes. And that was what made her own involvement with Clint so ridiculously futile.

Rose scrambled for the sunglasses she had hooked in her Rose Hill Farm co-op T-shirt and slid them on just in time to hide the sudden onslaught of moisture in her eyes. "I thought he'd changed his mind, that he'd come to see the value in them. Instead—" she swallowed around the lump in her throat "—it was just like it was with Barry. All along, Clint was paying lip service to what I desired while keeping his reservations to himself. Until suddenly I found out we don't want the same things after all."

"Clint's not interested in having kids and raising a family?"

The last thing she needed was her sister playing devil's advocate. "You know he wants that more than anything," Rose said, exasperated.

"Oh, then he doesn't love your kids?"

Rose pushed away the poignant memory of the five of them playing Superheroes together, of Clint reading stories to them while she made dinner, of him happily taking on the challenge to entice them to eat veggies again. "Actually, he loves them," she said thickly. And they all adored him, too.

"Then he doesn't love *you*," Violet presumed.

Wasn't that the gist of it? Because if he had, he would have been more than willing to meet her halfway and negotiate a happy ending for both of them. Rose wiped at a tear spilling over her cheek. "I guess not."

An awkward silence fell. "But you don't know for sure."

"How can I?" Lounging against the car next to her sister, Rose replied in a rush, "He never said he loved me." He wanted her. She knew that. Just as she wanted him. But was wanting someone and making love the same as loving someone in that forever-and-ever way?

Violet laid a gentle hand on her shoulder. "Did you tell him how you felt?"

"He knows I enjoyed spending time with him." *Making love with him.* "Working side by side with him…"

"Wow." Her sister snorted. "That must have rocked his world. Had him all ready to propose."

Rose glared at her, demanding, "Whose side are you on?"

Violet took her by the shoulders and forced her to listen. "Yours. And Clint's. Listen to me, Rose." This time, it was her voice that broke a little. "When I was with Sterling, I thought we had all the time in the world. I assumed he knew how much I cared about him by the way I looked at him and how passionately we made love. I mean, he had to know, right? So, for fear of sounding hokey or jinxing it in some way, I didn't say all the things I felt in my heart." Tears welling, she went on thickly, "And then the cancer got worse, he was fighting so hard for his life, and…I just never got the chance. Now I have to live with that regret every day, every moment of my life. You don't."

"But what if it was all just infatuation…and Clint really doesn't love me back? Or he sort of does, but he still thinks we're all wrong for each other?" She didn't want to put him on the spot only to have it all blow up in her face again.

"Then at least you'll know you tried." Violet folded her in for a long, sisterly hug. "Love is all about taking risks, Rose." She drew back to look into her eyes. "You've come this far. Why not go the rest of the way?"

"I THOUGHT YOU were going to mow the blackberry bushes down," Gannon said.

Clint went back to the tractor he'd all but given up on

but decided to resurrect. "Are you here to nag?" he muttered to his friend and neighbor. "'Cause if you are…"

"Grouchy, hmm?"

Clint scowled at him "So. Is there a reason for this visit?"

"Lily sent me to talk sense into you."

Clint wiped the sweat from his brow with the back of his forearm. "About what?" It wasn't like Rose's triplet to mind anyone else's business but her own.

"What do you think, knucklehead? Rose."

Clint removed the spark plug he'd just loosened. Like the others he had already removed, it looked fine. "We're over."

"Really? Because you still look like a lovesick calf."

Clint moved around to the other side of the engine. "Funny."

Gannon followed him lazily. "And Rose isn't looking any better, in case you're wondering."

Clint glared. "That didn't stop her from signing a contract with the tractor manufacturer." Without him. "And negotiating my release from further duties and responsibilities."

A small smile. "So you are keeping tabs on her."

More than he wanted to admit. Clint shrugged. "It was in the Laramie newspaper."

"Dallas, Austin and Houston papers, too. She also had a radio interview the other day that went particularly well. Did you hear it?"

He had, if only to savor the sound of her sweet, melodic voice. Clint went back to working on a particularly stubborn plug that was corroded to the base. "I'm happy for her."

"Just not interested in making her happy?"

Clint tossed his tool into the box and headed for the ranch house. He stormed across the porch, through the front hall and into the kitchen. Plucked two beers from the fridge and handed one to his ornery visitor.

He twisted off the cap, lounged against the counter and took a long, thirsty drink. "I'm not interested in fame and fortune. I want to ranch, not farm, and I want a quiet, satisfying family life on the Double Creek."

And he wasn't negotiating that, period.

"So, basically, it could be any woman and any children filling the bill, as long as they don't ask you to drive a berry picker."

Clint flexed his jaw, trying to keep his temper in check. But the truth was…his days driving that damn thing, with Rose close by, helping out, had been among the happiest days of his life.

He took another drink. "Obviously, I'd need to be attracted to whoever I marry."

"That's it?" Gannon asked with a lawyerly lift of his brow. "No love required."

Clint knew that, as one of the state's premier divorce attorneys, Gannon had seen his fair share of passionate relationships go bust. He had also witnessed families that had found a way to survive despite the odds.

Clint sobered. "Love would be great, if it happened."

Gannon studied him. "But it might not."

That wasn't the point. Not here anyway. "Rose thrives on adventure and excitement," he reminded the other man impatiently.

"All the McCabe women do. You can't lasso one unless you're willing to generate a few sparks."

He and Rose had done that all right. He'd never made love with anyone that way, with all his heart and soul. Never had a woman given back to him so completely, either.

A pain that had nothing to do with the physical stabbed his chest, in the region of his heart. Sorrow tightened his middle. "If I thought that were enough—"

"Did you ask her if it was?"

"What was the point when I'd already let her down just by planning to turn the best acreage on my ranch back to pasture?" He raked a hand through his hair. "She wasn't going to get past that, no matter what I did to try and lessen the impact."

"You didn't give her a chance to get past it."

"Because at the end of the day, the common financial interest in the blackberry harvest—" and a staggering amount of passion "—was all that we had."

He had hoped it was more. Rose's reaction, simply accepting his dictum instead of trying to meet him halfway and negotiate a solution—the way she would have with anyone else—had showed him that it wasn't more after all.

Gannon shook his head in exasperation. "If you think she wanted you only for what you could do for her professionally and financially, then you really are a fool. But the fact you still have yet to mow down even one of those berry bushes, even with a brand-new tractor sitting in the barn, tells me you know different—" he pointed to the center of Clint's chest "—in here." He paused to let his words sink in. "The real question is, what are you going to do about it?"

Rose had just slid the strawberry-rhubarb cobbler into the oven to bake when the front screen door slammed open. "Mommy! Mr. Clint is here!" Scarlet shouted from the bungalow's front porch.

Oh, no, Rose thought, grabbing a dish towel to dry her hands. Not now. Not yet! She wasn't ready for her big mea culpa.

Stephen bustled in, his little chest puffed out. "He says he's got somethin' for you."

"But he can't give it to you until you come outside," Sophia finished breathlessly.

Rose caught her reflection in the glass front of the microwave. In a pretty T-shirt and shorts, her hair and make-up done, she looked fine. It was just her heart that was ailing. Her vulnerability that made her want to stick to the best-laid plans, and not try to wing it again.

"Mommy," Scarlet reminded her, bossy as ever, "Mr. Clint is waiting!"

"Yeah." Stephen grabbed one of her hands.

Sophia held the other. "Let's go see him!"

In for a penny, in for a pound.

Rose took a deep breath and let the children lead her out to the porch.

Clint was standing there, handsome as ever. Recently showered and shaven, he wore an older, snug-fitting pair of dark denim jeans, boots, and the lucky shirt the triplets had nearly ruined before she'd erased the stains and brought it back to life. A tan Stetson slanted across one brow. He cradled a beribboned seedling in his big, strong hands. He looked at once hopeful and wary.

Her tension building, Rose could only stare at him.

"I probably should have called first," he said.

If their nearly two weeks apart had taught her anything, it was that she didn't want them to stand on formality. Ever again. He'd made the first move. It was up to her to make the second—even if this wasn't quite the way she had envisioned her apology to him.

Her heart pounding like a wild thing in her chest, she glided close enough to inhale the familiar leather and spice mixed with the masculine fragrance unique to him. Courage, she thought resolutely. If she could manage three kids on her own, she could certainly win Clint's love.

She smiled, ignoring the growing knot of emotion in her throat. "You can drop by anytime. In fact, I'm glad you did. I have one last check to give you for the blackberry harvest. I was going to mail it, but then I thought I should probably deliver it in person." Which was where the strawberry-rhubarb cobbler and babysitter she'd gotten for later came in.

He nodded, listening, oblivious to her plans. Not seeming to mind at all the way she was suddenly babbling.

He gave her another long, hesitant look, then hunkered down to the triplets. He held his arms out wide and encompassed them in a big, loving hug, which they returned with all their hearts. Finally they drew apart, and Clint gazed fondly down at them. "Listen, kiddos, do you think you-all could do something for me?"

The triplets nodded eagerly.

Like Rose, they were so lonesome for him, they were more than willing to comply with whatever he wanted.

"Could you-all go draw some pictures for me?"

They bounced up and down. "What kind?"

His grin widened affably. He gave them another brief, encouraging hug, then straightened with easy, masculine grace. "Anything you like."

They beamed, so pleased to have been asked.

Talk about a good idea!

"I'd like it if you could all draw one for me, too," Rose added, figuring that would give her and Clint at least ten minutes alone to talk and, ideally, make up. "Your crayons and paper are on the shelf in the family room."

"'Kay, Mommy!" The triplets raced inside, slamming the door in their wake.

Aware it was her turn to take the lead, Rose took a deep, bracing breath and tilted her head up to his. "I've been wanting to talk to you."

Clint set down the planter. "If you don't mind," he interrupted huskily, "I'd like to say what I need to first."

"Okay." Aware her knees were shaking, she sat down on the wide porch steps and buried her hands in her apron.

He settled beside her, taking her hand in his, his expression serious and intent. "A lot of what happened has been my fault," he confessed, looking deep into her eyes. "I knew you wanted me to keep the berry patch on the Double Creek, and that you thought I had changed my mind, even though I knew that I had no intention of doing that."

The strength of his touch imbued her with warmth. She turned to face him, her bent knee nudging his thigh. "Then why didn't you say something?"

Regret tightened the corners of his mouth. "Because I didn't want to do anything that would mess up what was happening between us. And I was looking for a way to save the day without sacrificing what I wanted for my land and my ranch." He lifted a hand. "You don't have to say it. I know how selfish that was."

His sober admission prompted a self-effacing one from her. "I was selfish, too. Wanting things only my way and no other." She sighed.

"We both made mistakes," he said, squeezing her palm. They had.

He reached for the planter he had set aside. "Which is where this seedling comes in."

Rose looked at it curiously. Without leaves, it was impossible to tell what it was. "I gather it's some sort of apology...?"

"Actually, a lot more than that," he murmured, placing it in her hands. "I've talked to Amy, and she is taking cuttings from all the blackberry bushes on my land. She's going to grow and sell them in her nursery. She also gave me an estimate of what it would cost to plant ten acres— or more, however many you want—of the Double Creek berries at Rose Hill, on some of your currently unused farm land. She thinks the optimum time for this would be in late October or early November, and I've told her that I will foot the bill."

"You don't have to do this."

"I want to. But in the meantime, this plant is what will be, I hope, the beginning of the planting and growing of even more Double Creek blackberries than the ones currently on my ranch."

"I don't know what to say." Throat clogged with tears, she realized he really did get it, that what was important to her *was* important to him, after all. She put the plant aside and turned to him, her hands outstretched.

His voice dropped a notch. "I also wanted to tell you I've changed my mind about doing the advertising campaign for the farm-equipment company. I agreed to keep the berry patch intact and let them film there next year, and every year after that, if they so desire." He paused for a brief moment. "In return, they've agreed to give us the berry picker and reinstate the discount on any future farm equipment we purchase. They've rehired me to do appearances with you, as they originally envisioned, with the two of us playing off our remarkable chemistry." He took her hands in his. "Of course, you'd have to agree to all of this."

She squeezed his fingers. "I will. But only," she kept her gaze locked with his and stipulated carefully, "on the condition we become friends again." Because she couldn't bear it if they weren't. And they had to start somewhere, if they were ever to recoup what they had enjoyed—and lost.

He pulled her to her feet. "Actually, I'd like a little more than that, Rose." His eyes twinkled with mirth. "And believe it or not, I'm even prepared to negotiate the conditions and parameters with you."

Rose admired the masculine planes of his face, the determined slant of his lips. "We don't have to strike a deal to be together, Clint. Especially since it was all my wheeling and dealing—" and her constant need to take both their businesses to the next level "—that helped break us up in the first place."

He brought her all the way into his arms and ran a hand

tenderly down her spine. "I know you like excitement and being in the thick of things."

She snuggled against his hard, strong body. "And I know you're a rancher, not a farmer, and that you like the quiet of wide-open spaces."

The need she felt was reflected in his gaze. "The fact we're opposites in a lot of ways, and just alike in others, is what makes our attraction so powerful. And it *is*, powerful, Rose," he concluded softly, bending his head to kiss her, sweetly and evocatively.

Tenderness wafted through her, fueling an even deeper reverence and need. "I know that," she whispered back, cupping his jaw in her hand. "But I'm also aware that you can't have a successful relationship unless both partners are willing to acquiesce to make the other happy. So—" she took another deep bolstering breath, meaning her next words with all her heart and soul "—if you want to mow down the berry patch and make it all pastureland, I'm okay with that. If you still want to give up on the ad campaign entirely, I'm okay with that, too. I'll even give my part up if—"

He cut her off with a Texas-size grin. "Actually, I like the idea of us working together. And playing together. And building a life and a home and raising a family together."

The tears she'd been holding back finally spilled over her lashes.

Eyes dark with emotion, he hugged her close, everything they had yet to say symbolized in that single move. He caught her against him, their hearts pounding in unison. He threaded his hands through her hair, pressed a kiss on her temple and gazed adoringly down at her. "I love you, Rose."

Everything she had ever wanted was suddenly hers for the taking. "Oh, Clint," she murmured joyously, "I love you, too. So much."

"And one of these days, when you're ready and your kids are ready, I want you to marry me."

"I want you to marry me, too." She marveled at the wonder of the moment, then sighed contentedly, teasing, "Perhaps sooner than you know."

He laughed out loud. "Is that a yes?"

Rose nodded and hugged him closer still. "You better believe it is!"

Epilogue

"I get to be in a wedding!" Stephen zoomed past.

Clint scooped the little boy up in his arms before he could run out into the chapel, where guests were gathering. What a difference six months could make. Rose's son had gone from complaining about anything and everything ceremony-related to sheer elation.

"Slow down, little fella," Clint chided fondly, bussing the top of his head before giving him an affectionate hug. "You have to save some energy for your trek up the aisle."

Stephen beamed and laced his arms around Clint's neck, looking as happy to be with Clint as Clint was to be with him. "I get to carry the ring on a pillow!"

"Yes, you do."

"And us girls get to carry baskets and sprinkle flowers," Scarlet announced, not to be outdone.

"And then you and Mommy are going to say 'I do' and put rings on and kiss and you'll be our daddy and we'll be a forever family," Sophia concluded.

Not that they didn't already feel like one, Clint thought on a wave of contentment. But it would be good to have it official, to have the whole world know how deep his commitment to Rose and the kids went, and vice versa.

Clint sat down on the bench in the anteroom, Stephen on his lap, the girls on either side of him. It was a scene that had been enacted many times, yet he never got tired of it. And never would.

"You-all look so nice today," he complimented them warmly. Stephen was in a black miniature tuxedo and pleated white shirt that matched Clint's. The girls wore dark green chiffon with ribbon sashes and big flouncy skirts, like the rest of the bridesmaids.

"Mommy is pretty, too," Sophia confided with a dreamy look on her face.

"But you can't see her yet," Scarlet warned. "Not until she comes down the aisle."

Clint smiled. "I can hardly wait." Not just to see his beautiful bride in her wedding finery, but finally to have Rose and the kids move into the Double Creek Ranch house.

They were going to use the bungalow at Rose Hill Farm, too, as an office for Rose and a small, cozy retreat when they all needed a change in scene, or simply to be closer to Rose's base of operations.

That way they'd be able to hold onto everything that meant so much to both of them and minimize the number of changes the kids went through, too.

In the chapel, the music started.

Clint realized on a satisfied exhalation that it was time.

Rose's five sisters filed into the anteroom. As previously arranged, they took charge of the flower girls and ring bearer. Gannon came to collect Clint. He and Clint and the groomsmen joined the minister. The ceremony started on a rush of excitement and joy. First the children and bridesmaids came down the aisle. Then Rose appeared on her father's arm. Clint met his bride's eyes. And in that instant, Clint lost his breath and his heart all over again.

In an ivory lace gown and tiara, Rose was not just gorgeous as could be. She was getting the wedding of her dreams. He was getting all of his wishes, too. A woman to love who loved him back just as fiercely as he loved her. A family. With, Rose had promised him the last time they'd made love, more babies to come. It would be impossible, he thought, to be any happier than they were at this very moment. By the time Jackson gave his daughter's hand in marriage, and Clint joined her at the altar and took Rose's hand in his, there wasn't a dry eye in the place. The wave of emotion built as they said their vows in clear, steady voices. It ended with a rousing cheer when the rings were on and he finally, exuberantly kissed his bride, cementing the union for all time.

"What do you think?" Rose asked hours later, when the reception had finally wound down. The two of them were getting in the limousine hired to drive them the short distance from the dance hall to the cottage on Lake Laramie, where they planned to honeymoon. She snuggled as close as the skirt of her wedding gown would allow and laid her head on his shoulder. "Were our nuptials everything you had hoped?"

"You're everything I ever hoped." Shifting her onto his lap, Clint buried his face in the fragrant silk of her hair and cuddled her close. She felt and smelled so good. Like a soft, warm field of wildflowers on a sun-drenched spring day. Like Rose...

He nestled even closer, aware she stole his breath, even now. He admitted gruffly, "But to answer your question, yes, they were. And then some."

He felt her lips curve against his throat. Saw her smile. "For me, too." She kissed his pulse and made it jump.

He smoothed a hand down her back, over the gentle slope of her hip. "Have I told you how much you mean to me?" he rasped. "How you've made every single one of my dreams come true?"

She loosened the bow on his tie, undid the first two buttons of his shirt and ran her fingers over his skin. "Only about a hundred million times."

Threading both hands through her hair, he tilted her face up to his and kissed her softly, evocatively. "Just so you know."

They drew apart. She gazed into his eyes for a long moment. "You mean the world to me, too," she told him tenderly.

"That's good to know," he whispered back triumphantly, kissing her once again with everything he had.

And their life together as husband and wife began.

* * * * *

Watch for the next book in the
McCABE MULTIPLES *miniseries,*
LONE STAR BABY by Cathy Gillen Thacker.

Coming September 2015, only
from Harlequin American Romance!

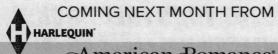

COMING NEXT MONTH FROM

HARLEQUIN®

American Romance®

Available July 7, 2015

#1553 THE COWBOY SEAL'S TRIPLETS
Bridesmaids Creek
by Tina Leonard
John Lopez "Squint" Mathison learned a lot in the Navy, but taming wild child Daisy Donovan requires a different set of skills. Skills he's going to need as an expectant father!

#1554 THE BULL RIDER'S SON
Reckless, Arizona
by Cathy McDavid
When newly hired bull manager and old friend Shane Westcott shows up at the Easy Money Rodeo Arena, Cassidy Beckett is forced to reveal the secret she's been keeping for six years: the identity of her son's father.

#1555 THE HEART OF A COWBOY
Blue Falls, Texas
by Trish Milburn
Natalie Todd has returned to Blue Falls with a terrible secret. She knows she must reveal the truth, but doing so will kill any feelings rancher Garrett Brody has for her...

#1556 A RANCHER OF HER OWN
The Hitching Post Hotel
by Barbara White Daille
Ranch manager and single father Pete Brannigan needs to find the right woman to make his family complete. And Jane Garland is completely unsuitable. So why can't he stop thinking about her?

YOU CAN FIND MORE INFORMATION ON UPCOMING HARLEQUIN® TITLES, FREE EXCERPTS AND MORE AT WWW.HARLEQUIN.COM.

HARCNM0615

REQUEST YOUR FREE BOOKS!
2 FREE NOVELS PLUS 2 FREE GIFTS!

HARLEQUIN®

American Romance®

LOVE, HOME & HAPPINESS

YES! Please send me 2 FREE Harlequin® American Romance® novels and my 2 FREE gifts (gifts are worth about $10). After receiving them, if I don't wish to receive any more books, I can return the shipping statement marked "cancel." If I don't cancel, I will receive 4 brand-new novels every month and be billed just $4.74 per book in the U.S. or $5.49 per book in Canada. That's a savings of at least 12% off the cover price! It's quite a bargain! Shipping and handling is just 50¢ per book in the U.S. and 75¢ per book in Canada.* I understand that accepting the 2 free books and gifts places me under no obligation to buy anything. I can always return a shipment and cancel at any time. Even if I never buy another book, the two free books and gifts are mine to keep forever.

154/354 HDN GHZZ

Name _____ (PLEASE PRINT) _____

Address _____ Apt. # _____

City _____ State/Prov. _____ Zip/Postal Code _____

Signature (if under 18, a parent or guardian must sign)

Mail to the **Reader Service:**
IN U.S.A.: P.O. Box 1867, Buffalo, NY 14240-1867
IN CANADA: P.O. Box 609, Fort Erie, Ontario L2A 5X3

Want to try two free books from another line?
Call 1-800-873-8635 or visit www.ReaderService.com

* Terms and prices subject to change without notice. Prices do not include applicable taxes. Sales tax applicable in N.Y. Canadian residents will be charged applicable taxes. Offer not valid in Quebec. This offer is limited to one order per household. Not valid for current subscribers to Harlequin American Romance books. All orders subject to credit approval. Credit or debit balances in a customer's account(s) may be offset by any other outstanding balance owed by or to the customer. Please allow 4 to 6 weeks for delivery. Offer available while quantities last.

Your Privacy—The Reader Service is committed to protecting your privacy. Our Privacy Policy is available online at www.ReaderService.com or upon request from the Reader Service.

We make a portion of our mailing list available to reputable third parties that offer products we believe may interest you. If you prefer that we not exchange your name with third parties, or if you wish to clarify or modify your communication preferences, please visit us at www.ReaderService.com/consumerchoice or write to us at Reader Service Preference Service, P.O. Box 9062, Buffalo, NY 14240-9062. Include your complete name and address.

HAR15

SPECIAL EXCERPT FROM

H HARLEQUIN®
™

American Romance®

*Daisy Donovan has finally decided to tell
John Lopez Mathison she loves him—but first she
must convince the people of Bridesmaids Creek
she's given up her wild ways!*

Read on for a sneak preview of
THE COWBOY SEAL'S TRIPLETS,
the fourth book in **Tina Leonard**'s *heartwarming
and hilarious series* **BRIDESMAIDS CREEK**.

Jane's gaze was steady on her. "John left town last night."

Daisy blinked. "Left town?"

The older woman hesitated, then sat across from her. Cosette Lafleur—Madame Matchmaker herself—slid in next to Jane, her pink-frosted hair accentuating her all-knowing eyes.

Daisy's heart sank. "He *couldn't* have left." He hadn't said goodbye, hadn't even mentioned he was planning to make like a stiff breeze and blow away.

The women stared at her with interest.

"Did you want him to stay, Daisy?" Jane asked.

"Well—" Daisy began, not knowing how to say that she'd thought she at least rated a "goodbye," considering she'd gotten quite in the habit of enjoying a nocturnal meeting in his arms. "It would have been nice."

"Have you finally realized where your heart belongs, Daisy?" Cosette asked, and Daisy started.

"My heart?" How was it that these women always seemed to read everyone's mind? A girl had to be very careful to keep her secrets tight to her chest. "Squint and I are friends."

Cosette winked at her, and a spark of hope lit inside her that maybe Cosette wasn't horribly angry or holding a grudge with her about the whole taking-over-her-shop thing.

"We know all about those kinds of friends," Cosette said, nodding wisely.

"Still," Jane said, "it does seem rather heartless of John to leave without telling you. Had you quarreled?"

Here it came, the well-meaning BC interference of which many suffered, all secretly cherished and she'd never had the benefit of experiencing. She had to say it was rather like being under a probing yet somehow friendly microscope. "We didn't quarrel."

"But you're in love with him," Cosette said.

"That may be putting it a bit—" Her words trailed off.

"Mildly?" Jane asked.

"Lightly?" Cosette said. "You are in fact head over heels in love with him?"

Daisy felt herself blush under all the scrutiny. Sheriff Dennis McAdams slid into the booth next to her, and the ladies wasted no time filling in the sheriff, who turned his curious gaze to her.

"He left last night," the sheriff said, and Daisy wondered if John Lopez Mathison had stopped by to see every single denizen of this town to say goodbye—except for her.

Don't miss THE COWBOY SEAL'S TRIPLETS
by Tina Leonard, available July 2015
wherever Harlequin® American Romance®
books and ebooks are sold.

www.Harlequin.com

Love the Harlequin book
you just read?

Your opinion matters.

Review this book on your favorite
book site, review site, blog or your own
social media properties and share
your opinion with other readers!

Be sure to connect with us at:
Harlequin.com/Newsletters
Facebook.com/HarlequinBooks
Twitter.com/HarlequinBooks

JUST CAN'T GET ENOUGH?

Join our social communities
and talk to us online.

You will have access to the latest
news on upcoming titles and special
promotions, but most importantly,
you can talk to other fans about your
favorite Harlequin reads.

Harlequin.com/Community

f Facebook.com/HarlequinBooks

t Twitter.com/HarlequinBooks

p Pinterest.com/HarlequinBooks

HSOCIAL

THE WORLD IS BETTER WITH
Romance

Harlequin has everything from contemporary, passionate and heartwarming to suspenseful and inspirational stories.

Whatever your mood, we have a romance just for you!

Connect with us to find your next great read, special offers and more.

f /HarlequinBooks

🐦 @HarlequinBooks

www.HarlequinBlog.com

www.Harlequin.com/Newsletters

HARLEQUIN®

A *Romance* FOR EVERY MOOD™

www.Harlequin.com

SERIESHALOAD2015